BEAUTIFULLY MOVED

CANDIED CRUSH #5

CHARITY PARKERSON

—Warning: This book is intended for readers over the age of 18.

INTRODUCTION

TWO MEN OPPOSITE IN EVERY WAY. ONE UNFORGETTABLE NIGHT. NO GOOD CAN COME OF THIS.

Everyone knows Xavier's name, face, and body. Not only is he considered one of the world's most beautiful men, he hosts a popular cooking show in the buff. He's flawless... on the outside. Inside, Xavier is jaded and spoiled. He's used to having his way with whoever he chooses. No one has ever told him no. That's why he was beyond sick of everything before Dean came along. Dean isn't like anyone else. He ignores Xavier unless Xavier forces Dean to look his way. Xavier is intrigued. He can't stay away. It's too bad Dean keeps running from him.

Dean isn't anything like Xavier. He works a normal job, looks like a normal person, and gets shot down more often than not. It's not that he doesn't realize Xavier is completely flawless. In fact, he has a hard time not staring at Xavier all the time like a lunatic. The thing is, Dean isn't interested in getting crushed by some guy way out of his league. It's obvious Xavier is only looking for a distraction. It's laughable to think they could end up together. Until they spend one magical night together, that is.

After a single night in heaven, Dean runs for the hills, leaving Xavier baffled. Now Xavier has to do something he's never done before. He has to do the chasing if he hopes to win Dean. If not, he'll lose the only person who has ever made him feel any spark for life. Luckily, losing isn't a word Xavier knows.

ONE

"WILL YOU STAY AFTER THE SHOW?"

"I don't know. Is there a reason you're asking?"

"You know there is."

Dean couldn't stop running the conversation through his mind. Did he know why Xavier had asked him to stay after today's show? That was a loaded question, even for himself. Dean had met Xavier Nilsson months earlier when Dean's older brother Brett had been in an accident. Until then, Dean hadn't known Brett had a world renowned celebrity chef slash famous actor slash Sweden's most beautiful man temporarily living under his roof. It turned out Xavier was Brett's neighbor and his house had been under renovation until last week. Dean hadn't known Brett spoke to any of his

1

neighbors, much less moved one in. He thought Brett was too busy to talk to anyone... including Dean. Not that it mattered now. Xavier had moved back home last week and was now back to filming his nude cooking show in his own kitchen.

That was truly unfortunate, since once Dean learned Xavier had been staying with Brett, he hadn't been able to stay away. He had never visited his brother so much in his adult life. Honestly, he was more than a little surprised Brett hadn't called him on it yet. Goddamn, though, Xavier was beautiful. Platinum hair and gray eyes. He had an accent that made Dean want to taste the tanginess of it. Xavier never wore clothes. That definitely made him harder to ignore. Even on his show, *Cuisinier Unveiled,* Xavier cooked while wearing nothing but an apron. He continuously flashed the camera his bare ass, keeping the ratings high. Dean would know. Since he had met Xavier, he hadn't stopped watching the show. This was his first time seeing it live, though. The only reason Dean had been invited to today's taping was Brett's man Roman was cohosting and had used the opportunity to propose. It had been sweet. There had been tears and such.

Roman's proposal was the only sweet thing about the day. Every other second had been nothing but Dean and Xavier exchanging heated glances every chance they could. That brought him back to his original thought. Did he know why Xavier asked him to stay after the show? It was true that Xavier constantly made veiled sexual advances. Dean had never taken them to heart. He had to be that way. Dean couldn't let himself entertain the idea Xavier actually wanted him. Dean was the younger brother of a celebrity YouTube producer. That was it. Dean was not special in any way. And still, his amazing brother had given up so much for him. It was important that Dean stay contained and disciplined. Dean needed to be worthy of his brother's sacrifices. He needed not to need anything else. That was the only way he could make up for taking away Brett's family.

"You stayed."

Dean glanced around. Everyone else was gone. Goddamn it. He had stayed. "You asked me to, but didn't tell me why. I suppose curiosity killed the cat."

Xavier's gray eyes flashed with humor. He motioned toward the meal they had created on the show. "Someone needs to eat all this food, since everyone else ran away. Will you join me?"

That was the last offer Dean expected. He didn't

think there was any way he could say no without sounding rude. "Oh. Yeah. I guess."

A teasing smile touched Xavier's lips. "Which is it? Yeah or you guess?"

Dean took a breath before he said anything he couldn't take back. "Yes, I'll join you."

The triumph in Xavier's smile almost made Dean run for his life. Then, Xavier turned around, flashing his bare ass again as he grabbed a bottle of wine and two glasses. "You can't have Cavatelli and Mussels without white wine."

Dean snagged a stool at the kitchen island where all the food was displayed and sat. "I wouldn't know. This is my first time trying this. I don't eat a lot of shellfish."

Xavier kept his gaze locked on his task of pouring a glass of wine for Dean. "Is that because you don't like shellfish or because you don't know how to cook it properly?"

Dean shrugged. "I guess I'm a bit simplistic. It's just me, so there's no need to get fancy and cook a huge meal. In fact, I'm guilty of eating super unhealthy because it's just easier. It seems crazy to cook for only me."

After passing the glass Dean's way, Xavier fixed him a plate. "This is my job, so it's like a free pass to be wasteful. Which reminds me, I don't think I've heard what you do."

"I'm a tattoo artist," Dean said, accepting the plate.

Laughter filled Xavier's eyes, making them twice as gorgeous. "That explains all the ink on your hands. Did you do those yourself?"

Dean glanced at the clocks tattooed on the backs of his hands and the word "time" that was inked across his knuckles. "Yeah. I get bored sometimes."

"And you have time on your hands," Xavier said with a laugh, proving he understood the humor behind the designs.

Dean chuckled. "Yeah. They're a solid opening for a bad joke whenever anyone asks me for a favor."

"You don't laugh enough," Xavier said, jumping topics and taking Dean's breath. "It's a nice sound."

To hide his discomfort, Dean took a bite of his food. Flavor exploded across his tongue. Dean hadn't known what to expect, but it was delicious. "Wow. This is amazing."

Xavier sipped his wine while watching Dean eat. There was so much heat in his eyes, Dean felt a bit subconscious. It didn't help Xavier wasn't eating. He simply watched Dean's every move with an intensity that had the hair standing on the back of Dean's neck.

Xavier set his glass aside. "May I ask you a question without you running for the hills?"

Dean's brow furrowed. "Why would you expect me to run? Do I strike you as skittish?"

"Not skittish. More mulish, I suppose. You don't like me, so I worry if I ask a question you consider untoward, you might wash your hands of me."

Dean pushed his plate aside and polished off his wine. This conversation had taken a turn and needed his full attention. "It's not that I don't like you. I guess I just don't think we have much in common and I think of you as being more my brother's friend than mine. That doesn't mean I don't like you."

"Good." Xavier drained his glass. His stare transformed, making Dean's heart beat a little faster. "Have you ever kissed a man?"

"I'm sorry. What?"

Xavier motioned at Dean's body in general. "You are very much a man's man, which lends itself to a general vibe that you're straight, but I don't think you are completely set on women. So, have you ever kissed another man or not?"

Dean blinked several times, trying to wrap his mind around Xavier's claims. He wasn't used to people being so blunt. Dean also couldn't decide if he was meant to be insulted or not. "Um. No."

"But you've considered it, right?"

"You're very straightforward with your questions."

Xavier pulled a face like Dean confused him. "Why wouldn't I be? Prudishness is a very American trait. I've lived here a long time and still haven't adjusted to that aspect of society. Like clothes, for example. I'm in the comfort of my home. Why should I dress? Everyone is always so covered at the beach. Why? It's hot. I don't understand why everyone is so ashamed of their bodies. It's just skin. As to sexuality, so many people here think it's one way or the other. Either you're straight or gay. That's ignorant. Life has so many fun shades. Why do Americans shy away from their desires? It's baffling."

Even though he found Xavier's approach a bit abrasive, he had to agree. He hadn't ever dated a man, but that didn't mean he was opposed or didn't find other men attractive. Dean just didn't think he would appeal to men. He didn't look like his brother. Dean wasn't tiny and perfectly styled. He was thick and hairy. Dean tried to stay decently clean cut, but he had hair on his chest and liked to eat. He didn't fit with a certain crowd, or any crowd, for that matter.

Dean was just some guy. Still, he didn't like being thought of as prudish. That wasn't true.

"Yeah. I've thought about kissing men."

Xavier cocked his head to one side and eyed Dean. "You're what? Twenty-five? Why haven't you tried it before now?"

Dean's mouth went dry. "Before now?"

Xavier circled the island. Dean found himself turning on his stool to face Xavier, unable to take his eyes off the man. His heartbeat thumped in his ears as Xavier moved to stand between his knees. His hands slid up Dean's thighs while his gaze never wavered from holding Dean's stare. "I said what I meant. Before now."

All Dean could do was watch and hold his breath as Xavier inched closer. As he spread his knees farther apart, making room for Xavier, Dean realized he had already decided his fate. When his hands slid up Xavier's forearms, Dean accepted he wanted this more than he cared to admit. He didn't know what to expect, yet Xavier still surprised him. He didn't move fast. His lips touched the corner of Dean's mouth lightly before pulling away an inch. Dean swayed toward him. Xavier brushed noses with Dean as he changed directions. This time, he gently sucked Dean's bottom lip.

Dean's hands found Xavier's hips, he pulled Xavier closer. Xavier's tongue traced the seam of Dean's mouth. Dean opened and Xavier took control. He held Dean's face and explored his mouth. Dean's body reacted like Xavier licked his cock rather than his tongue. His fingers found the apron's ties and tugged. The material dropped to the floor. Xavier's kiss deepened. Dean squeezed his ass, trying to get even closer. Xavier was soft yet firm. Dean couldn't stop touching him. His heart beat so fast, he worried it might fail. Then Xavier's kiss softened. He spent a moment brushing lips with Dean before backing away.

Xavier's cheeks were flushed, his eyes hooded. His gaze lingered on Dean's mouth. "There. Now you can never again say you haven't kissed a man." His gaze lifted and collided with Dean's. "What's next?"

Dean arms shot out, stopping Xavier from getting away. He wanted Xavier's mouth on his skin. Dean hauled Xavier back into his arms. "It's time for you to stop teasing me. That's what."

The evil-sounding chuckle that fell from Xavier's lips told the truth. Xavier had one hundred percent been tormenting him on purpose for months now.

His hands went straight for the button on Dean's jeans. "I want to taste your dick."

Dean's lungs nearly collapsed as all the air left him in a sharp pant. He had never had anyone this incredibly sexy say something so freaking hot to him. If Dean wasn't careful, Xavier would have him blowing in thirty seconds flat. Xavier set Dean's erection free like a master. He dropped his head to Dean's lap without preamble. All Dean could do was grasp at his sanity while Brett deep throated him like a fucking star. Pressure beat at his crown. He was ready to fill Xavier's mouth full of cum in a matter of seconds. Dean didn't want things to end that fast. He had spent way too many nights with his cock in his hand, stroking and chanting Xavier's name. He needed more.

Dean snagged Xavier's hair and tugged. He stood as he urged Xavier's mouth back to his. He tried beating his desire into submission while he explored Xavier's mouth. "I want to fuck you." The confession was easier to say than to execute to Dean's mind. He craved being inside Xavier, but this was his first time with a man. He had no clue where to start.

Xavier took control—like he understood Dean's plight. "Tell me you carry a condom."

Dean nodded and dug for his wallet. His hands

shook as tore into the square package. Adrenaline and lust made it hard for him to focus, but he didn't miss a second of watching Xavier use some type of cooking oil to lube his asshole. He was shameless. Xavier held Dean's stare while fingering and stretching himself. It was hot. Dean wasn't used to dealing with someone who unabashedly took what they wanted.

While Dean watched, Xavier stroked his cock. He looked every bit as turned on as Dean felt. "Take off your shirt."

Dean immediately obeyed.

"Mhmm. Goddamn. Look at that hairy chest and all that ink. Fuck. You are delicious." Xavier leaned back against the island. With his elbows braced on the hard surface behind him, Xavier's abs bunched as he easily lifted his weight. Dean was fascinated by the sight of Xavier's muscles in action, showing off his balance and strength. He wrapped his legs around Dean, urging him closer. "Don't worry. You won't hurt me. If you do, I kind of like that."

Fuck. Dean really wouldn't last long. Xavier did and said all the right things to make Dean's dick throb. "I don't think I've ever been so hard for anyone."

Xavier smirked at Dean's confession. "Prove it."

Dean couldn't pass up that challenge. With one hand gripping Xavier's firm ass cheek, Dean used the other to guide his dick to Xavier's asshole. The tight muscles surrounding Xavier's hole fought him. He had to push his way inside. Once his crown was in, Xavier's body sucked him deeper. A loud pant escaped Dean. He hadn't expected that. He was so horny, he thought—even if he came in two strokes—he would just keep going until he pulled a second orgasm. Dean wanted this too badly to stop.

The moment Dean was fully seated, their gazes collided. Xavier looked every bit as aroused as Dean felt. His mouth lifted in one corner. "You can never again say you haven't been with a man."

Xavier's taunt hit hard. Until the words were spoken, Dean hadn't accepted how badly he had wanted this. Craved it. Needed it. He squeezed Xavier's ass and thrust, going deeper and harder than he intended. Xavier moaned. He looked like being on Dean's cock was ecstasy. Something inside Dean broke. He thrust again, falling into a hard rhythm, and fucking Xavier the way he liked it—rough to the point of violent.

Xavier never protested the treatment or wavered in strength as he held himself balanced against the island. Sweat rolled down Dean's skin as he fought to reach orgasm. He slammed inside Xavier over and over again. The sound of slapping skin and moans fills the kitchen.

Dean's balls drew up tight. He felt the slow crawl of pressure rising in his cock before pounding against his crown. He leaned into Xavier, determined to blow. When his orgasm finally hit, Dean's knees quaked, forcing him to lock them against the waves of pleasure that poured through him. As he let Xavier's feet slip to the ground, a horrible realization overcame him. Xavier hadn't come. Dean couldn't have that. Maybe this was his first time, but he couldn't leave anyone disappointed, especially someone as far out of his league as Xavier.

His entire body was like gelatin. He didn't think. Dean just reacted. He dropped to his knees and licked Xavier's erection from root to tip. A sense of fuck it overcame him. He liked getting his dick sucked. Just because he had never blown anyone didn't mean he couldn't figure it out. Dean knew what he liked. It stood to reason Xavier would like similar things. He wrapped his lips around Xavier's crown and sucked. A loud moan caressed his ears, so Dean did it again. With each approving noise Xavier made, Dean took him a little deeper into his mouth. Before he knew it, he bobbed on Xavier's dick, sucking and tugging. The more Xavier squirmed; the more Dean enjoyed himself. He felt Xavier tense. Dean sucked harder and faster—like he raced toward his own orgasm. Xavier's body jerked. Salty fluid filled Dean's mouth. Out of pure instinct, he swallowed. He was immediately dehydrated—like swallowing ocean water, but he still wanted to pat himself on the back. He hadn't disappointed Xavier. That was something.

Xavier urged him back to his feet and claimed his mouth. This kiss was different. Almost lazy. It tempted Dean to stay all night. "Stay a little longer," Xavier said, sounding like a siren luring Dean to his death.

"Okay." Dean heard his agreement like it came from a distance. He didn't recognize himself. Being with Xavier was the most surreal experience of his life. Dean didn't want it to end. Even though he knew all good things must come to their inevitable conclusion, this had been this best night of Dean's life. He would never forget it, but he also wouldn't repeat it.

TWO

BRETT: *COFFEE AT THE BACK PORCH AT 9?*

Dean: *I'll be there.*

Since Dean had gone from seeing his brother almost every day to not seeing him at all in the past month, he couldn't ignore a coffee date with him. Plus, The Back Porch had a great selection of brews. Not to mention, he had always liked the people who frequented the popular coffeehouse, even though he never went there unless he was with Brett. Dean ended up being ten minutes early. Sometimes, gauging L.A. traffic was impossible. As he walked through the door, Dean realized this would be his first time stepping inside alone. Heads turned his way. A few familiar faces smiled and nodded. Dean returned the gesture. He nearly breathed a sigh of relief as the manager, Dawson, approached him.

"Hey. I don't think I've ever seen you without your brother."

"He's on his way."

Dean had always thought Dawson looked like a nice person. He had sweet-looking brown eyes and he focused on people when they spoke to him—like he cared what they had to say.

Dawson was no different today. He nodded. "I have a small table, perfect for two, open in the back corner. Will that work?"

"That's perfect. Thank you."

With a nod, Dawson led him to the only open table in the place. "Here you go. Would you like to go ahead and order or are you waiting on Brett?"

"I'll wait for Brett. How have you been, by the way?" Dean asked as he sat and set his helmet on the table.

Dawson shrugged. "Not bad. I've been working a lot more since Wrecker got married, so there's that."

Dean's eyebrows tried crawling to his hairline. "Wrecker got married?"

A bright smile lit Dawson's face. "How did you not know that? Even I saw it on the news and I never watch TV. Plus, the wedding was here, so it wasn't like I could miss it."

Discomfort had Dean trying hard not to fidget. "Like you said, I'm never here without Brett and he's been busy, so I miss a lot." Dean had no idea if the part about Brett being busy was true. He had avoided Brett's place like it was haunted by a poltergeist since his night with Xavier. Dean couldn't chance running into the too-hot-to-handle chef. Once was a good time. Twice was a recipe for looking desperate on Dean's part. He did not want to end up on the news for stalking.

Dawson motioned toward the empty chair across from him. "Do you mind if I keep you company until Brett arrives?"

"Of course not, but I don't want to get you in trouble."

With a snort, Dawson sat. "Don't worry about that. Wrecker needs me. He doesn't care what I do as long as this place keeps running efficiently in his absence. May I ask you a question?"

Dean felt like nothing good ever started that way, but he could hardly say no. "Sure."

"Is there a reason you never come here unless you're with Brett?"

A smile snapped to Dean's lips. "It's definitely

not because I think you'll bite, if that's what you're thinking. This place is way out of my way. I live across town."

Dawson's eyes swam with laughter. "I definitely do bite, but I'm glad to know that's not what's keeping you away. It's too bad we're out of your way. I like seeing you around."

There was no missing the interest in Dawson's voice. He was nice. In fact, Dawson possessed all the qualities Dean should be looking for in a man. Dean let a hint of interest show in his tone too. "Maybe I'll try to make the drive a little more often."

"Hey guys. Am I late?"

Dean's gaze snapped to his brother as Brett appeared beside the table. As usual, he was dressed like pimping wasn't easy, making Dean smile. "Nah. I was early." He glanced Dawson's way for a second. "I'm glad I was."

With a blush, Dawson stood so Brett could sit. "What can I get started for you two?"

"Black coffee for me," Brett said as he claimed the seat Dawson vacated.

"Same," Dean said when Dawson's gaze slid his way.

"Two easy-to-please men. I like that. I'll be right back with your order."

Dean flashed Dawson a grateful smile before he got away and then focused on Brett. "How have you been? You look great."

Brett's dark blue eyes flashed with irritation. "I'm glad to see you still think flattery solves everything when I haven't heard from you in a month."

Dean hid his guilt by turning the tables on Brett. "You have my number and know where I live. I haven't heard from you either."

"Not true. I texted you this morning. Plus, you know what I'm getting at. I know you get busy at your shop and I never want to interrupt an appointment. But, for a while there, I saw you every day, and then you just stopped coming around the minute Roman asked me to marry him. Do you feel unwelcome now or something? It's still your home."

Shit. Dean hadn't thought of the timing. Roman had asked Brett to marry him on the same day Dean found himself inside the most beautiful man on the planet. Dean's stomach cramped with desire at just the thought of Xavier. If he was this big of a mess after one time with Xavier, he couldn't imagine what seeing the man again would do to him. Dean scrambled for a plausible lie. "I've been busy trying to keep the shop afloat. By the time I close up every day, it's too late to drive all the way across town for a short visit before making the trip home."

Brett didn't look appeased. "You're the one who wanted the house and shop on the other side of town. I tried buying you a place in the same neighborhood, or hell, you never had to move out. It's not like you need to work. I'm glad you do, and I'm proud of you, but you're the one who chose to move as far away from me as you possibly could while staying in the same town."

Dean fought the urge to rub his temples. He shouldn't have brought up the distance between their homes. Dean hadn't been thinking. This had always been a sore spot for them. When he had decided to move out three years ago, at first, Brett had been hurt. Once he had accepted that Dean wanted to be independent, he had tried buying Dean a home in the same neighborhood worth millions. Dean didn't want that. He needed to make his own way, but he had also realized he needed to compromise with Brett. So he had let Brett buy him a tiny house in a regular people neighborhood on the other side of town. Brett hadn't given in easily. Now, Dean realized too late, he shouldn't have used the distance as an excuse. Before he could find a way to backpedal, Xavier appeared.

"I apologize for my lateness. Two guys stopped me in the parking lot. I'll admit they made me a delicious offer, but I'm much more tempted by what sits at this table." He grabbed an empty chair from the closest table without asking if it belonged to anyone. The three guys at the table didn't stop him. They were too busy staring at Xavier, openly star struck. Xavier set the chair as close to Dean as possible, trapping him. He filled the seat, draped his arm across the back of Dean's chair, and settled in like claiming his place. "Hello, sexy. You've been hiding from me."

Dean glanced around, floundering. He didn't know how to react. Brett hadn't said Xavier was coming too. Dean said the first thought that came to mind. "I can't believe you're dressed." And it was sexy. Goddamn. Xavier looked like a man who needed to be stripped bare and fucked hard. While his jeans and shirt weren't anything that would have stood out on anyone else, it was Xavier. He made everything look ten times sexier than normal.

Xavier flashed a laughing gaze his way. "The last time I saw you, I thought you rather enjoyed having my naughty bits bare."

Unfortunately, Dawson chose that moment to bring their drinks. He set Dean's coffee down harder than necessary and refused to meet his stare. "Does anyone need anything else?"

Dean tried to get Dawson to look his way, hoping to reassure him. "Thank you. I'm good."

Xavier took a cautious sip of Dean's coffee. As he set the cup back down, he kissed Dean's cheek. "That's not bad. I'll have one of those as well."

Giving up, Dean pinched the spot between his eyes. Dawson walked away without a word. When Dean reopened his eyes, he found Brett's gaze moving between Xavier and him. His expression said everything Dean needed to know. Brett wasn't dumb. In fact, he was the smartest person Dean knew.

"I have questions."

"Please don't." Even Dean heard the dead note to his voice. Dean had been trying so hard to stay away from Xavier. He couldn't let himself believe Xavier's attention was anything more than boredom on Xavier's part. Dean had definitely one hundred percent never wanted Brett to know about them.

At Dean's plea, Brett picked up his coffee and started sipping like his life depended on the hydration.

Xavier didn't seem to notice or care about any discomfort. He kept talking and making things worse. "Did you ask Dean why he's been avoiding us?"

Dean sighed. "I haven't been avoiding anyone."

"He's says he's been working," Brett said at the same time. Brett set his coffee aside. "I'm sorry. I tried, but I can't do it. How long has this been going on and why did neither of you tell me?"

"A month," Xavier said at the same time as Dean said, "There's nothing going on."

Brett look between them. "Which is it? A month or nothing is going on?"

A cup of coffee appeared on the table in front of Xavier. Dawson was gone again before Dean could even look his way. Maybe it was for the best. Dean couldn't blame the guy.

Xavier didn't comment on the service. He stayed focused on the task of telling Dean's business—like Brett wasn't a brother who had raised him like a father. "We slept together a month ago, but he's been avoiding me ever since. So, possibly, it's both. This has been going on a month and nothing has happened since, because he's been avoiding me."

Brett didn't look like he could stop studying them. His gaze kept moving from Dean to Xavier and back again—like a fan stuck on oscillate. "I have more questions."

"Please don't," Dean said again, losing his temper. He was uncomfortable and no one seemed to care how he felt. Brett had never seen Dean with a man and he knew that was the biggest shock for Brett at the moment. For Dean, he didn't care how anyone else felt at the moment. That one night with Xavier had been just for him. It was supposed to be a magical memory. Dean pushed away from the table and stood, leaving Xavier no choice but to move his arm from Dean's chair. He snagged his helmet from the table. It took some doing, but he managed to shove his way out from behind the table.

"Dean."

Dean ignored Brett. He couldn't explain his anger, but the rage was there. Before he made it to the door, Dean spotted Dawson wiping down a nearby table. He changed directions and pulled out his wallet. Dean found a twenty and passed it Dawson's way.

"For my drink. I'm sorry about earlier." Even Dean heard the pain lacing his voice.

A hint of shock crossed Dawson's features as he reached for the bill. Dean didn't stick around to hear a response. He had to get out of there. No one understood. Dean wasn't a part of this crowd. Just because Brett had fame and money, that didn't mean

24

it extended to him. Dean was a nobody. Nobodies were playthings to people like Xavier. Dean wanted to be with someone who thought he was special. Someone like Xavier could never think Dean was anything more than a good time. A shot of pain hit him, nearly taking him to his knees as an image of Xavier kissing a path down his chest flashed through his mind. Dean had never wanted anything in his life more than he had yearned for that night they spent together.

He straddled his bike. Dean didn't move. He needed to get to work, but everything hurt too bad. The urge to turn around and see Xavier's face one more time was slowly murdering him. If he ached this much after one night together, he would never survive two. He sat straddling his motorcycle and incapable of moving. Every molecule of his body stayed focused on the memory of Xavier in his arms. Dean couldn't even lift his arms to put on his helmet. When strong fingers gripped the back of his neck, Dean gasped. It was his fantasies coming to life again. The moment of confusion Xavier created by pulling Dean from the fantasy of him and into the real thing was enough time for Xavier to claim his mouth.

Dean didn't think. He forgot where they were

and where he had been intent on going. Xavier had caught him while he had been trapped somewhere between a frothy rage and ecstasy at the memory of Xavier. Something in Dean's chest expanded as Xavier's tongue stroked his and the man's hand slid down his arm, caressing. Damned if Xavier didn't taste like he cared.

Xavier pulled away.

Dean found himself staring into gray eyes that seemed to look into his soul.

Xavier swiped the back of his knuckles down Dean's cheek. "I'm sorry that being with me embarrassed you." He walked away before his words penetrated the haze he created around Dean's brain.

As Dean looked on, Xavier climbed behind the wheel of an oddly nondescript black SUV. He didn't give Dean time to decide if he would go after him. Xavier pulled from the lot without looking back. Reality came rushing back like lightning. He had just been kissed by one of the world's biggest celebrities in the middle of a public parking lot. There was no taking that back. Xavier thought Dean was ashamed of what they had done. Nothing could be further from the truth. Dean had never regretted anything less in his life. That was why he thought things should end there. He didn't want to taint the only perfect memory he had by trying to push for more. This was for the best. Xavier would forget him soon enough. Everyone forgot Dean. Xavier would see. By next month, he wouldn't remember Dean's name.

"I hear you had an interesting, if not short, coffee date this morning."

Xavier looked up from his laptop as Roman cleared the kitchen doorway. He went back to working on his menus. It never surprised him when Brett or Roman appeared without knocking. He always left his back door unlocked for them. "Perhaps it was of interest to Brett. Other than an amazing kiss in the parking lot, it was not that great for me. But yes, it was brief."

Roman snagged an empty chair at the table. "I can't believe you're dressed."

"It happens on occasion," Xavier said absently.

Roman sneaked a quick peek at Xavier's computer screen. "Work? Do you usually sit at your kitchen table to work? Don't you have an office in this ginormous house?"

"Yes, but it's too far from the refrigerator and pantry, which would have me making too many trips between my office and here, cross checking my list to my menus and recipes." Xavier focused on Roman again. "Did you need something?"

"Not really. I just wanted to check on you. Brett said you seemed upset when you left the coffeehouse this morning."

"Why would I be upset?"

Roman shifted in his seat, looking uncomfortable, and making Xavier's guilt skyrocket. He knew he was being difficult.

Xavier sighed and closed his laptop before taking off his blue-blocking glasses. "Look. You can tell Brett not to worry. Our friendship is in no danger. Dean is obviously embarrassed by what happened between us, and—really—I should've seen that coming. So there's no fear I'll make him have to stop talking to me because I've hurt his brother, or whatever."

Roman cocked his head to one side and eyed Xavier. "Is that really what you think Brett's worrying about?"

Xavier shrugged. He already felt like a big enough idiot. He wished they could stop talking about this. "It doesn't matter. I obviously miscalculated the situation. It won't happen again. There's no need to continue this discussion."

Roman leaned his elbow on the table and propped up his chin on his fist. "Are you saying it'll never happen again because there's no hope or because you don't plan to try?"

Despite his best efforts, a small growl escaped Xavier. "Does it matter?"

"Actually, yes," Roman said, sounding as if it was the simplest thing in the world. "Now that I'm with Brett and we're getting married, I've slowed down. My past looks a lot clearer now. I don't regret my missed opportunities because everything in my life led me to Brett, but I see now where I let my ridiculous thoughts hold me back. There were so many times I didn't go after things because I didn't want to get hurt or I felt like it was inevitable that I would get publicly smacked down. That's dumb as hell. I probably missed hundreds of chances at happiness because staying in my comfort zone was easier. If you really like Dean, and—judging by watching you two interact, I think you do—you're making a mistake if you quit now."

Xavier shook his head. A chuckle rose in his throat. "Are you saying Brett is worried I'm missing a shot with his brother?"

"Oh, no. Brett is one hundred percent certain

that Dean will break his own heart to keep himself from dating anyone with money."

Xavier's forehead furrowed. He hadn't expected that. "What?"

Roman nodded. "Brett and Dean's parents stopped talking to them when Dean was fifteen. Brett finished raising him. Brett thinks that Dean feels like it's his fault and like he cost Brett their parents. So he's determined to live life as humbly as possible, like a penance or something. He doesn't think he deserves anything good. Brett thinks you would definitely fall under the too good to accept category. He's worried about you both. I am too, because I think Brett's right, and I also think you're so used to having your way that you'll give up at the first hint of a challenge."

Xavier's eyebrows tried crawling to his hairline. "Wow. That's a real asshole thing to say to your friend who is also your boss."

"Am I wrong?"

Was he? Xavier didn't know. He had been so busy since walking away from Dean trying not to think or feel that he hadn't examined the facts. Unfortunately, he had done nothing but think about his situation since Dean left after their night together and didn't look back. He had never questioned himself like this before. Had he pushed too hard? Misread the signs? Had he done something Dean didn't like? In the end, it didn't matter. The results were the same. Dean had walked away and not looked back. Seeing him again today had only proven Xavier's worst fears. Dean wanted nothing else to do with him.

Xavier stood and moved to the refrigerator. He needed buttermilk for one of next week's recipes. There was some in the fridge, but it didn't look like enough.

Roman blew out a loud breath. "Fine. Do what you want, then."

Xavier didn't stop hiding inside the fridge until Roman left. His heart dipped a little lower once he was alone. Xavier had gotten a bit used to living with Brett while his house had been under renovation. Now he got lonelier than he liked to admit. At Brett's, Dean had visited every day and Xavier had lapped up the attention. All of Xavier's family still lived in Sweden. He worked from home these days and barely spoke to anyone besides Brett and Roman. Seeing Dean every day had been nice. Xavier had enjoyed the teasing and flirting. The lingering eye contact. Now everything felt quiet. Empty.

As Xavier moved back to the table, he noticed a lone paper sitting on his closed laptop. He picked it up and eyed the scratched words. A small smile tugged at his lips. Roman had left him Dean's cellphone number, address, and the address of where he worked. The ball was in his court, it seemed. Maybe he had a little time for some light stalking. After all, he truly did like Dean. It seemed crazy to give up now.

THREE

WITH HIS FOOT RESTING ON AN EMPTY STOOL, Dean stared sightlessly at a magazine from the stool beside it. Some nights, work could be boring as shit. Other nights, it felt like he couldn't breathe because he was too busy. It looked like tonight would be one of the endless ones where nothing happened. Dean flipped back to the magazine's cover to remind himself what he had been staring at for the past hour. He didn't think he had absorbed any of it. Oh yeah. It was some rock legend thing.

"Wow. I haven't been by in a while. You've got a lot more sketches up."

Dean tossed his magazine aside and stood. As he looked on, Brett flipped through a few of the poster board display cases, checking out Dean's designs. "I haven't been sleeping much. That gives me extra time to draw. Plus," he motioned at the empty room. "As you can see, I'm not exactly crawling with business."

Brett's gaze snapped his way. His forehead furrowed. "Do I need to pay for a billboard or something to get some traffic headed your way?"

Dean fought a smile. Brett's heart was always in the right place. "No. I'm still getting enough business to get by. It's just the slow season right now. People are hibernating. When spring fever hits and they start thinking about showing skin, I'll be too busy to think."

With a nod, Brett crossed the room. "Your talent never ceases to blow me away."

A smile pulled at Dean's lips. "We're a talented family."

"Damn right, we are." Brett leaned his elbows on the counter. "Are you still mad at me?"

Dean immediately returned to being the little brother who had the greatest big brother in the world. "I was never mad at you. I don't know how to explain what I'm feeling. It's not anger, though."

A sweet smile touched Brett's lips. "Embarrassment after Xavier put all your business on display?"

Dean shook his head. "Why does everyone keep accusing me of being embarrassed? I'm not. I mean, it's Xavier. Anyone would be flattered."

"He's the one who should be flattered," Brett shot back, transforming into the overprotective brother. "As far as I've seen, you've never given another guy the time of day. Xavier should feel fucking honored to have gotten your attention, even if it was only for one night."

"I like him." Dean didn't mean to admit that. It was too late to take it back. He needed to talk to someone. "He's your friend, so I know you know this already, but he's annoyingly irresistible—like I don't want to like him, but I do."

A guy came through the door before Brett could respond. He set an insulated food container on the counter. "Which one of you is Dean?"

Dean moved closer. "That's me."

The guy pushed the box Dean's way and handed him a note. "Enjoy." He walked away without a backward glance.

Dean's gaze moved Brett's way before returning to the container. A delicious smell slowly filled the air. Dean slipped the note card from inside its envelope and read aloud. "You're not allowed to go hungry on my watch—X."

A bright smile lit Brett's face. He straightened away from the counter. "You're right. He's irresistible. I'll leave you to your dinner. Don't be a stranger, okay? I've been worried I did something wrong."

No one guilted quite like Brett. He liked to sneak attack, so Dean felt horrible for not visiting while trying to avoid Xavier. "I'll come by tomorrow. You have to update me on all the wedding plans."

The way Brett smiled reminded Dean how incredibly happy Brett had been since falling for Roman. "I will. See you tomorrow." With a final wave, Brett headed out, leaving Dean alone with his food.

Dean slid the insulated container closer and unzipped the top. He popped the tabs on the rubber lid and lifted it away. It was lasagna. Dean's stomach growled. There was silverware included that looked expensive. Dean had a bad feeling he would have to return the dish and cutlery to its owner. That meant seeing Xavier again. The food smelled too good for him to be angry. He grabbed a drink from the mini fridge beneath the counter and settled in to eat. The first bite was like heaven. Dean wanted to savor every bite, but he scraped an empty plate before he knew what happened.

He stared at the empty surface disappointed. Dean had never had noodles quite like those. They had almost melted on his tongue like butter. Xavier was such an amazing cook. It was probably a good thing they weren't dating. Otherwise, Dean would be the size of a house in six months. He had always been the type to gain weight easily, which was funny only because Brett could get blown over in a strong wind. Weight never stuck to his brother's bones. In some ways, it was like they weren't related at all. In others, they were exactly alike. They had the same color hair, but Brett looked like their dad while Dean looked like their mom. Even though they both had blue eyes, Brett's were dark, whereas Dean's were light. By looking at them, Dean didn't think anyone could tell they were brothers.

With a sad sigh, Dean popped the rubber lid back in place and zipped the container closed again. He had a feeling he would think about that lasagna from time to time. Damned if Xavier didn't tempt him to get his heart broken. The bright red insulated dish sat on the counter, taunting him all night. Even as he did a few tattoos and cleaned up the shop, his gaze kept sliding its way. Five minutes before closing time, Dean made up his mind. He would return the dish tonight before he changed his mind. If he left it on Xavier's front porch, he would know he had done the right thing without having to actually see Xavier. Since he didn't have Xavier's number, he could easily leave a thank-you note with the dish and not feel guilty.

As Dean headed toward the door to lock up, it opened. Xavier stepped through, looking like something from a magazine. His platinum hair was swept up and back, perfectly styled. Black pants molded his skin. A white shirt with too low of a neckline showed off a hint of the man's chiseled chest. Dean's mouth went dry. His stomach muscles tightened with longing.

Xavier smiled like he couldn't be happier to see Dean. "The Mad Tatter has to be the greatest name for a tattoo shop ever. When you told me you're a tattoo artist, you didn't tell me you own your own place. I had to hear that from Brett."

"I'm closed." Dean didn't know what else to say. He was too shocked at Xavier's sudden appearance.

Xavier's smile didn't dim. "I'm aware. That's why I waited so late to come by. I didn't want to disturb you while you were working."

Dean fought the urge to close the distance between them and take the kiss that belonged to him. In fact, his gaze dropped to Xavier's mouth, as if judging the distance to his prize. He forced himself to turn away.

Dean snagged the dish from the counter. "I believe this is yours." When he turned to hand Xavier the plate, Xavier stood much closer than Dean expected.

"What did you think?" Xavier asked as he took the container and set it back on the counter.

Dean blinked, trying to keep up with the conversation while Xavier stood too close. "I think you're insanely talented and I have nothing to offer you." Horror washed over Dean as he realized what he said. It was too late to take it back and Xavier turned away before Dean could see his reaction.

Xavier eyed the sketches on the wall. "Did you do all these?"

"Yes." Dean's gaze never wavered from Xavier.

With a nod, Xavier moved closer and inspected the details. "That's amazing."

A smile snapped to Dean's lips. "Are you in the market for some ink?"

Xavier flashed a smile over his shoulder. "Maybe not tonight." He turned Dean's way. "But there's no one else I would choose, if I wanted one. Truthfully, I've just never pictured myself with a tattoo."

Xavier always entranced him, making Dean say

every thought in his head. "Yeah. I suppose you are a flawless canvas."

To Dean's surprise, Xavier's smile fell. Something unnamed passed over Xavier's features. "I guess I should let you go home. You're probably tired."

As Xavier reached past him again for the plate, realization struck. Xavier had probably never been seen as anything but a pretty face and sexy body. While that was a hell of a boon for someone in Hollywood, it would likely get old when it came to relationships and meeting people. Dean hated the idea that he might be treating Xavier exactly the way everyone else did.

"What do you do for fun?" Dean asked before Xavier could get away.

"Yoga."

Okay. Dean wasn't doing yoga. "Anything else? Like, do you go to the movies or do you like to play video games? What do you do for entertainment?"

Xavier's expression cleared, as if he realized Dean tried to find a connection. "I don't usually go to the movies, since I would get mobbed, but I do have an awesome home theater and I do like video games."

Dean would take it. "How do you feel about horror films?"

"I've played in a few, so I enjoy them."

"Would you like to see one with me? I don't have a huge home theater and I'm kind of the artistic nerdy and boring type, but I like you. Not Xavier Nilsson the international superstar or whatever, but you."

Xavier's lips turned up into a sweet smile. "I am Xavier Nilsson the international superstar."

Dean blew out a sigh. Xavier was impossible. Sometimes, Dean caught a glimpse of a real person inside him. Otherwise, he was so goddamn cocky and conceited that Dean didn't know how to connect with him. "I don't know what you want from me."

Xavier's smile grew. "It was a joke. I like you too, and I would love to watch a movie with you."

Dean's irritation slipped away, only to be replaced by a slight nervous flutter in his gut. He had truly only meant to spend one night with Xavier. Now, things didn't feel quite so cut and dry. "Okay, I guess—if you're ready—you can follow me home," Dean said, heading for the door.

Xavier fell into step behind him. "Okay."

Dean took measured breaths all the way through locking up and walking to his motorcycle, while trying hard not to look Xavier's way. He couldn't stop himself from flashing Xavier a shy smile as they parted ways. Dean straddled his bike and prayed he wasn't making a mistake. Then his gaze slid Xavier's way one more time and he wasn't sure he gave a fuck. For whatever reason, Dean had Xavier's attention for now. He didn't know how to stop wanting the guy, so Dean wouldn't try. There were worse ways to get crushed, he supposed. Dean imagined he would find out soon enough.

———

WHEN XAVIER HAD SHOWN UP AT DEAN'S business, he hadn't known what to expect. He hoped sending Dean something to eat first would soften his welcome. The last thing Xavier expected was to get invited back to Dean's place. Yet, here he was.

Dean's house surprised Xavier. It was a tiny brick home with brown shutters that probably wasn't more than thirteen hundred square feet. It also wasn't in the nicest neighborhood. The guy's brother had a mountain of money. Brett loved Dean. Xavier couldn't imagine Brett letting Dean live in a place so small. Then again, Xavier thought about the way Dean hadn't backed down when Xavier kissed him that first time. It wasn't likely anyone let Dean do anything.

Dean motioned toward a leather loveseat. "Have a seat."

Xavier crossed the room and sat. The buttery soft and expensive material welcomed him, contouring his body. A smile tugged at Xavier's lips. Apparently, Brett hadn't let Dean go without some luxury.

"Would you like a beer?"

"Sure." Honestly, Xavier didn't give a shit what they did. He just wanted to be close to Dean. Xavier didn't know why. He had met countless men over the years. There was nothing special about this one, except... maybe there was, because Xavier wanted more. From Xavier's spot on the couch, he could see Dean moving around inside the kitchen. He grabbed two bottles of beer from the fridge and headed Xavier's way. Xavier's gaze never wavered from Dean. He ate up the sight of Dean closing the distance between them.

Dean held one of the bottles out to Xavier. Xavier took a steadying breath as he accepted the drink and Dean filled the spot beside him. He sat close, invading Xavier's space. Dean held Xavier's stare as he turned up his beer. Xavier swore his body vibrated in response to the heat in Dean's stare. "What movie are we watching?" Xavier needed to talk about something. Otherwise, he would end up jumping on Dean and humping his yummy body. He loved that hairy chest and soft stomach. Dean looked like a man who liked to eat. He was perfect. Xavier loved to feed people.

Dean set his beer aside. "Do you really want to watch a movie?"

A surprised chuckle burst from Xavier. "My, my, Dean. Did you lure me here under false pretenses?"

A flash of doubt crossed Dean's features. "No. I'm not that guy. There's a movie that came out last—"

Xavier kissed him, cutting off Dean's words. He paused long enough to set his beer aside and take Dean's away to do the same. Then, he straddled Dean's lap and reclaimed his mouth. Their tongues stroked like they had missed each other. Xavier pulled away again and stole Dean's shirt. He needed to feel of that chest hair and belly he had been thinking about nonstop for the past month. Xavier ran his hands over every place he could reach while trying to lick the roof of Dean's mouth. He was ridiculously happy to be here. Their kiss slowed as their fingers linked. Xavier realized they were toying with each other's hands—like they were equally incapable of not touching each other.

Dean cupped the back of Xavier's neck and

stroked. Something tightened in Xavier's chest. Dean pulled away enough to touch his forehead to Xavier's. He looked winded and soft—like he felt something for Xavier. No one knew how badly Xavier wanted that. No one was more surprised by that than him, but he wanted Dean's heart.

"I like you a lot."

Xavier smiled at Dean's confession. "You're so brave. Damn, it's sexy. I like you a lot too."

Dean brushed a sweet kiss across Xavier's cheek. "I'd love for you to stay and watch this movie with me—like a real date. Are you genuinely interested in that or are you killing time with me?"

"If I was only killing time with you, you never would have seen me again after our night together. I'd very much like to see more of you." Xavier licked his lips nervously. He couldn't back down now. "Like a boyfriend would."

A soft chuckle fell from Dean's lips. "You're fulfilling a lot of firsts for me. No one has ever asked me to be their boyfriend. I like the sound of that. Honestly, I like it a lot."

Xavier had a hard time breathing. Desire had him in a chokehold. Not to mention, he had no idea what he was doing. Dean messed with his head a little. "You should definitely kiss me again to seal the deal."

Dean slowly lured him closer. Xavier held his stare, dragging out the anticipation. He loved Dean's rough kiss. In fact, he enjoyed it a bit too much. That was how he knew they needed to give this a go. Everyone else, he could take them or leave them. Dean was different. Xavier wanted to show him all the things Dean had never tried with anyone else. As their lips met, Xavier found himself sinking deeper into Dean's hold. He would watch this movie and try to behave, but afterward, Xavier would have his way. He could wait a couple of hours. Xavier had the patience of a saint.

"Fuck it. We'll have plenty of chances to watch a movie," Dean growled as he flipped Xavier onto the couch and covered his body.

Laughter burbled in Xavier's throat.

Dean covered his mouth, cutting off the sound. He tore at Xavier's clothes, going to work and stripping him. It wasn't hard. While Xavier's clothes molded his body, he always only wore expensive clothing that was partially spandex. Its lightweight, no-pressure texture was the only material he could stand against his skin. As Dean peeled Xavier's pants off and realized Xavier wore no underwear, a sexy growl vibrated from him. "Goddamn, you're sexy." He licked Xavier's crown on his way to completely removing Xavier's pants.

Xavier's back arched. He openly writhed. Dean was manly and carnal. It was sexy as hell and pushed all the right buttons with Xavier. He scratched at Dean's skin, trying to drag Dean back to his lips. Xavier wanted Dean inside him.

"I want you to take it how you want it this time," Dean said, tugging Xavier from the couch and onto the floor so he straddled Dean's hips. "You didn't come the last time I was inside you. I want you to come this time."

Xavier had never been hit so hard by anyone. He was used to men taking what they wanted from him during sex. If he came, he came. If he didn't, then it was up to him to finish things off. Dean wasn't like that. Last time, he had dropped to his knees. Despite never sucking anyone's dick before, Dean had done that for him to ensure he came. This time, he demanded Xavier do things his way.

Xavier cast a quick look around the room. "Do you have condoms and lube around here?"

He felt Dean's sudden disappointment like it was a physical thing. "Fuck. There's a condom in my wallet, but I don't keep lube."

He tugged at Dean's pants, peeling them off. Xavier refused to let that ruin things. "Get the condom. Do you have baby oil, coconut oil, or anything like that?"

Dean brightened. "Yes. In the kitchen."

Xavier pressed a quick kiss to Dean's chest. "Put that condom on, sexy. I'll find the oil." Xavier jumped to his feet and headed for the kitchen. It was a small white space with decent appliances. Xavier tried not to get distracted by Dean's overly organized cabinets. That was fucking hot. He found the coconut oil and shamelessly lubed up before returning to Dean. He found Dean still on the living room floor nude, hard, and stroking himself. Xavier's dick twitched. Pre-cum rolled down his length. He couldn't explain it, but Dean made him hornier than anyone ever had before. Xavier didn't waste any time. He quickly crossed the room and straddled Dean's body. As he stood over Dean with one foot on each side of Dean's hips, Dean's expression softened. He ran his hands up Xavier's calves.

"You are incredibly gorgeous. I must be the luckiest guy on the planet."

A chuckle that sounded evil even to his ears escaped Xavier. "You're about to be," he said, dropping to his knees. He scraped his teeth across

Dean's nipple. Dean hissed. Xavier reached between their bodies and palmed Dean's cock. He held it in place as he sat back, letting the erection penetrate him. His head fell back, and his eyes slipped closed as Dean's dick filled him to overflowing. The pressure bordered on painful. He loved it.

"Fuck. You look so goddamn sexy on my dick."

Xavier's eyes opened. He stared down at Dean as he lifted and impaled himself again. He kept changing angles until he found the perfect spot. The angle that made him moan. After a minute of getting that internal button stroked, Xavier lost all semblance of going slow. He slammed himself against Dean's cock, riding him hard, and taking what he wanted. Dean panted and moaned, making sounds like a man who enjoyed getting fucked, so Xavier didn't slow. He tugged at his dick when the madness became too much. He loved the anticipation, but he wanted the payoff. Pressure built, threatening to snap his mind. Xavier tugged and rocked. He wanted everything. Dean felt so good.

"That's it, sexy," Dean praised, sounding turned on. "Fuck me. Take it. Take what you want. Goddamn. I didn't know it could be this good."

Ecstasy punched Xavier in the dick. An orgasm

ripped from him, sending cum flying. He shook it out all over Dean's body, taking pleasure in the way it wetted Dean's skin.

Dean's fingers dug into Xavier's hips. He held tight and rolled, pinning Xavier beneath him. The air left Xavier's lungs as Dean slammed inside him. Skin slapped skin as Dean punished Xavier's asshole, ruining him for all others. Xavier fought for purchase. There was nothing to hold on to as Dean fucked him across the floor. Finally, Xavier slapped his hands down on the hardwood and pressed through his palms, rooting himself through his hands the way he did in yoga. He used his strength to keep them in place while Dean plowed forward. Dean was everywhere, licking every place he could reach while using Xavier's body.

Pressure started climbing Xavier's cock again. He held his breath, trying to ignore the sensation. Xavier had never come twice in one sexual encounter and he didn't want to get left hanging when Dean came. Xavier's body refused to be ignored. The harder he tried to pretend he wasn't dying to blow again, the worse the situation became. He closed his eyes and breathed. Dean cried out and slammed hard inside Xavier one final time. He could feel Dean's cock twitching inside him. The disappointment started to build, even though he knew that it was ridiculous.

Dean claimed his mouth. He stayed firmly seated in Xavier's ass. While they kissed, Dean reached between them and massaged Xavier's aching cock. A low moan rose in Xavier's throat. He tried to stay still. Xavier wanted Dean's semi hard dick to stay put. Dean's touch was almost teasing, forcing Xavier to stay completely focused on every stroke. His muscles tensed as he fought to reach a second orgasm with Dean barely moving his palm against him. A pant escaped as the pressure built. His hips lifted a hair, seeking more. Dean refused to tighten his hold. Xavier thought his mind would snap. A growl burst from him.

Dean chuckled against his lips.

Xavier buried his fingernails in Dean's skin, punishing him. Dean's touch lightened even more. Xavier thought he might scream in his frustration. Then, Dean's grip tightened.

"Come."

At Dean's demand, Xavier's body snapped like a spring coiled too tight. His muscles shook as an orgasm rocked his soul. All he could do was gasp and twitch in Dean's arms. He stared at Dean in awe as his body glitched and soared. No one made him feel the way Dean did. Xavier couldn't explain this. He didn't know what was happening between them, but he wasn't going anywhere until he figured it out. They were amazing together. Xavier wanted this. He wanted more.

FOUR

Xavier: *I WAS SITTING HERE, WAITING FOR YOU TO come home, and I was thinking. Have you always been an amazing artist, or did you learn it somewhere?*

Dean: *I have no formal training, if that's what you're asking. In fact, I wasn't very good in school. My head was always in the clouds and I was always in trouble for drawing rather than working. I used to take a lot of beatings for that before it was just Brett and me.*

Xavier: *Beatings? Like... should I hire a hitman?*

Dean: *You're sweet. No. Maybe I shouldn't have said beatings. More like I got chased in a circle while getting whipped with a belt.*

Xavier: *How is that better!?*

Dean: *LOL! I miss you.*

Xavier: *I miss you too. Come home soon.*

DEAN: *DO YOU WANT TO GO OUT TO EAT tonight?*

Xavier: *I've already cooked.*

Dean: *Okay. Sounds great.*

Xavier: *I didn't tell you what I made.*

Dean: *You made it. It's great.*

Xavier: *You're great.*

XAVIER: *DID YOU MAKE IT TO MY PLACE YET? I'M almost done with this meeting.*

Dean: *I'm here. In bed. Waiting.*

Xavier: *Yum. Are you nude? Hard? Thinking about me?*

Dean: *I'm thinking I need to hold an intervention for you. You have more pillows than any man alive. Every time I stay the night, I swear they've multiplied.*

Xavier: *LOL! I like fluffy things. I also love hard things so be ready.*

Dean: *Yes sir.*

Xavier: *You should let me cover a second artist at your shop. I'm spoiled and I want my teddy bear.*

Dean: *I'm almost done.*

Xavier: *Hurry or I'm jacking off in your bed.*

Dean: *God. You're such a tease.*

Dean: *I miss you so much. You make me wish I didn't have to work.*

Xavier: *Give me ten minutes. I'll come hang out with you there.*

Dean: *You don't have to do that. I don't want you to be bored.*

Xavier: *I'm good at making my own entertainment. You'll see.*

Dean: *Damn. I'm so fucking happy being with you. You're amazing.*

Xavier: *The feeling is mutual. Ten minutes.*

If there had ever been a time that Dean smiled as much, he couldn't recall it. Being with Xavier made him happy. They did everything together. To Dean's surprise, they were a lot alike. They both liked to stay home and watch TV. Xavier loved to cook, and Dean loved to eat. There were a few things they didn't share a love for, but Dean tried. Xavier worked out religiously—mostly doing some hardcore yoga. Dean liked to watch, so they found their common ground there. He let Xavier talk him into trying some easy poses. For the most part, Dean loved watching Xavier twist his nude body into some impossible-looking positions. Everything about Xavier made him hot. Dean was exactly where he feared he would be if he gave in to Xavier. He was completely snagged. Thankfully, Xavier seemed to be too. He genuinely believed Xavier was every bit as happy in their relationship. For Dean, it was like a dream come true.

"Your brother dropped a wedding invitation by my place this morning."

Dean nodded. He was barely awake. It had been a long night at work since business had picked up, but he was never too tired for Xavier. "Yeah. Some guy is supposed to come by the day after tomorrow and fit me for a custom tux or whatever, since I'm

Brett's best man." He stroked Xavier's stomach. Dean couldn't get enough of touching Xavier's soft skin.

"I'm hearing this will be some real fairytale type shit—like Brett is pulling out all the stops for Roman."

Dean snuggled closer, spooning Xavier as hard as he could. Sometimes, he couldn't get close enough to the man to suit his heart. He brushed his lips across the side of Xavier's neck. "Brett loves him. He wants to give Roman the world."

"You sound really tired. I'll let you sleep."

A smile tugged at Dean's lips. He never wanted to move. His lips found Xavier's nape again. "You're not bothering me. I love the sound of your voice."

He felt Xavier shrug. "Still. You worked tonight and I know you're tired. Go to sleep."

Dean closed his eyes and felt himself sinking. The warmth of Xavier's back against his chest snagged Dean's attention again, keeping him from falling asleep. "Xavier?"

"Yeah?"

Dean couldn't stop smiling at the way Xavier whispered—like trying not to bother him. "I like you."

"I like you too." He could hear the happiness in

Xavier's voice. Dean's heart swelled. He tried harder to fall asleep. It wasn't happening. He was just too damn moved by being with Xavier.

"Xavier?"

"I'm still here," Xavier said, sounding like he bit back his laughter.

"I like you a lot."

Xavier snorted. "I like you a lot too."

Dean bit his bottom lip, trying to stop smiling. He needed to go to sleep. It was late and he had a few early morning appointments. No matter how hard he tried, Dean couldn't stop turning over the last three months in his head. They had been the best months of his life. Dean wished he could express his feelings, but there seemed to be no words strong enough for the constant pressure in his chest. Asking Xavier to come back to his house that night had been the best decision of his life. Every day, Dean woke up and wondered if he should pinch himself. People like him definitely didn't land people like Xavier, but he had.

"Xavier?"

This time, Xavier didn't try to hide his laughter. His body shook with it. "Yeah?"

"I think I more than like you."

With a loud sigh, Xavier rolled until he faced

Dean. He tossed his leg over Dean's hips and scooted even closer. "You're not going to sleep, are you?"

"I'm trying."

Xavier brushed his lips across Dean's. "Are you? Are you really trying?" He kissed Dean again, robbing Dean of any hope of answering. Love built in Dean's chest. He really wanted to say the words, but he got the impression Xavier wasn't ready to hear them. That was okay. Dean could wait. They were together and Dean was damn proud of what they were building.

As Xavier lightly stroked Dean's every line and kissed him like they had all the time in the world, Dean's muscles finally relaxed. Xavier hypnotized Dean with his touch, slowly luring his brain into a peaceful hum. By the time Xavier settled into Dean's arms again, Dean's eyes were heavy, and his breathing slowed. He was with the person he was meant to be with. Dean felt that in his gut. He finally drifted off, accepting the peace only Xavier brought to his life. Tomorrow was another day they would be together. He was home.

Xavier stared at the ceiling, wide awake. His mind raced. Even though he didn't want to believe it, Xavier was pretty damn certain Dean had been moments away from telling Xavier he loved him before falling asleep. Xavier eyed Dean's sleeping form while beating back a panic attack.

Dean rolled away, setting him free. Xavier's throat burned. He needed to think. Xavier needed space. He couldn't think with Dean so close. While Xavier knew he cared about Dean, he didn't know if he was ready to exchange I love yous. They hadn't been dating that long. It wasn't that Xavier expected they wouldn't last or whatever, but I love you was huge. It was bigger than he expected at this point.

Xavier slipped from the bed and started silently dressing. He kept one eye locked on Dean, hoping he didn't wake him. Xavier wasn't sneaking away. He just needed a little space. For the past three months, he had been going with the flow, but he hadn't really considered where this thing was headed. The L word made things real. Love meant people got hurt. Dean's brother was Xavier's friend and neighbor. If Xavier hurt him, he would lose two people. Fuck. Dean's brother was marrying Xavier's cohost. That was three people. He had a lot to lose if they didn't work out. Shit. He couldn't breathe.

Without looking back, Xavier practically ran for it. The farther away he got from Dean's bed, the lighter he felt. He really just needed to think. Xavier knew he wanted to be with Dean. In fact, he was happier than he had ever been in his life. But happiness didn't really last that long in Hollywood. People didn't really fall in love here. Hell, Brett had found Roman in Aspen. If that didn't prove people didn't fall in real love in L.A., Xavier didn't know what did. He didn't want to lose Dean. Xavier knew that much. Why couldn't they stay the way they were? They were happy and uncomplicated. It felt like society was always pushing people to be more. Everyone they knew had been getting married lately. That put an undue burden on relationships like Dean and his to be more than they currently were. Xavier wanted to keep seeing Dean every day, the way he had been, but I love you. He didn't know about that.

Before Xavier realized it, he pulled into his garage with no memory of the actual drive. It amazed Xavier he hadn't killed anyone on the road. Xavier pulled the keys from the ignition and stared at nothing. He shouldn't have left. Dean made him happy. At the end of the day, that was all that mattered. They had been seeing each other every day for three months and Xavier couldn't get enough of Dean. Xavier never wanted to lose him. He had panicked. Xavier was an idiot. He wouldn't go back tonight and risk waking Dean.

Dean had been buried in work lately, starting his day extra early and keeping the shop open well past closing. Xavier saw how hard Dean worked to keep his business open. He refused to let Brett help and he hadn't been open long enough to bring more artists on board. Xavier didn't know how to make Dean's life any easier other than to let him sleep. If Dean wouldn't let Brett help, he sure as hell wouldn't let Xavier do anything. Dean was fiercely independent. A smile tugged at Xavier's lips. Everything about Dean turned him on and made him happy. They were amazing together.

Xavier's smile fell. Nothing but a cold and empty bed waited for him inside. Ugh. Sometimes, Xavier was his own worst enemy. Tomorrow, he would make this right. He would buy Dean some expensive wine and make a special dinner. They would be perfect. Dean would see. Xavier wouldn't be weak again. He wouldn't let him down.

XAVIER HAD ALREADY LEFT FOR THE DAY BEFORE Dean woke. After a moment of confusion, Dean remembered Xavier was scheduled to appear on Coral Live, a popular morning talk show. Dean shouldn't have been surprised Xavier needed to leave early to beat rush hour while headed downtown. He sent Xavier a quick text, wishing him luck before he got moving. Dean had a full schedule too. Spring fever had fully set in and he had back-to-back appointments scheduled for the entire day. In fact, he had to open early today for a regular who had several hours penciled in for a full back piece.

Dean rushed to get ready and forgot to check his phone to see if Xavier responded. It wasn't until an hour into working that Dean checked his watch. "Do you mind if I turn on the TV?"

Wendy flashed him a smile over her shoulder. "Sounds great. It'll give me something else to focus on beyond the scratching at my skin."

Dean jumped to his feet and grabbed the remote. He couldn't miss Xavier being on Coral's show. Dean had already missed the first ten minutes, since he had lost track of time. He already felt sick over missing his good morning kiss. Dean still couldn't believe he hadn't heard Xavier leave, but he had been extra tired lately.

A smile pulled at Dean's lips as Xavier's image filled the screen and his voice filled the air. Damn. Dean hadn't expected to fall so hard so fast. Or maybe he had. After all, he had recognized Xavier as a danger to his soul from the very beginning.

"So, Xavier, do you have a natural aversion to wearing clothes or is the studio paying you Gates bucks to cook in the buff? Either way, we're not complaining. Unless it's about you having to wear pants today."

The audience laughed. Dean ducked his head to hide how bright his smile had become. He was thankful he was working on a back tattoo. That gave him some freedom to bask in his happiness. He was ridiculously proud to be dating Xavier.

Xavier's sexy laughter rumbled through the TV. "Actually, I suffer from a condition called Sensory Processing Disorder. While I obviously can wear clothes, it's very uncomfortable. When I'm dressed, my mind is always split between whatever I'm doing and the misery of being dressed. I'm overly aware of every place my clothes are rubbing. It's like my brain itches, and I can't scratch it. I'm just lucky someone is willing to pay me to do what I love in the buff."

Dean's heart twisted in his chest at the confession.

He hadn't known that. Xavier had never said a word. All the times Dean had forced Xavier to stay dressed, he had practically been torturing the man. Dean felt terrible. He would have to call him later and apologize. Dean loved Xavier's naked body. He didn't care if Xavier never wore clothes again. Xavier's admission made Dean realize how much they still didn't know about each other. He would have to work harder at their relationship. Xavier deserved better.

Coral's voice turned wicked—like she planned to get personal. "There's another question my viewers are dying to know."

"Hit me with it."

Dean chuckled at Xavier's tone. He truly sounded like he had zero secrets.

"I polled my audience yesterday, asking people to send in their questions for you. One question was asked ninety percent more than any other. Are you dating anyone?"

Dean found himself pausing his work to stare at the TV. He couldn't explain his sudden nervousness. They did everything together. Their relationship wasn't a secret. This just seemed different. Xavier stood in front of the world. This felt like a public declaration. After today, everyone would know Dean dated men. To be specific, he dated an extremely famous and sexy man.

"Sorry to disappoint your audience, Coral. I'm still single. No gossip to share there. You know I'm boring."

Dean blinked. The air left his lungs in a whoosh, as if he had been punched in the chest. Surely he hadn't heard what he thought he heard. He grabbed the remote and pressed the back button, returning to thirty seconds earlier. "Sorry to disappoint your audience, Coral. I'm still single. No gossip to share there. You know I'm boring."

Dean flinched. He could barely breathe. His eyes burned. He passed the remote to Wendy. "You can find something else to watch, if you want."

She set the remote out of his reach. "Are you kidding me? This dude is fine as hell. He's number five on my hall pass list."

Even though Dean didn't feel it, he chuckled and went back to shadowing her tattoo. He tried not to listen to anymore. Dean had definitely heard enough. It seemed Xavier hadn't been gone this morning because he had a talk show to do. Dean had scared him away by almost dropping the L word. He should have known better. Xavier had always been too good to be true. What the fuck had he been thinking? Someone like Xavier didn't fall in love. Still, Dean couldn't believe Xavier would just walk away without telling Dean to his face that they were over. He thought Xavier was braver than that.

"What are your plans for the future?"

Despite his best efforts, Dean found himself listening again at Coral's question.

Xavier made the sexy humming noise that Dean loved so much and chill bumps rose on his skin. He was like Pavlov's fucking dog and he hated it. "Well, as you know, I have a movie coming out next month. I play a cop with a drug addiction who is being blackmailed by a mafia boss. Hopefully, it's a hit."

Dean focused on breathing. With every word Xavier spoke, Dean was reminded of the distance between them. Xavier was this famous guy who never should have looked Dean's way. Dean had gotten caught up in the fantasy of Xavier. He was no better than Wendy's imaginary hall pass list. Dean had thought he was special, but he wasn't.

"What about your parents? I know they still live in Sweden and I'm sure they're very proud. Do you have plans to return?"

"That's always been my plan." Dean froze at the words. His gaze slid back toward the TV. He couldn't look away as Xavier hammered the final nail in their coffin.

"When Hollywood is done with me, I have a place in Sweden waiting."

Dean wondered if he would hyperventilate. There had never been any hope for them. This entire relationship had been a waste of time. For a moment, Dean couldn't move or catch his breath. He was paralyzed with pain. His throat hurt.

"Are you okay?"

Dean shook himself from his inner meltdown. "Yeah. Sorry. I've been battling a massive headache."

"If you hand me my purse, I have some Tylenol."

Dean tried for a smile. "Thank you, but I've already taken something. Don't worry about me." He couldn't believe how the lies rolled from his tongue. It seemed getting dumped on live TV made him into a professional storyteller. Dean focused on Wendy's back and got to work. Once again, this place was all he had. He would do well to remember that in the future. No more sexy men. No more dreaming. No more happiness. No more Xavier. The story of Dean's life.

FIVE

Xᴀᴠɪᴇʀ ʜᴀᴅ ꜰᴀʟʟᴇɴ ᴀꜱʟᴇᴇᴘ ᴡᴀɪᴛɪɴɢ ꜰᴏʀ Dᴇᴀɴ to call. Normally, Dean called him when he closed up shop and they made plans for where they would sleep for the night. This morning, Xavier had woken up to a bright sun and no missed calls. First, he had tried texting Dean. When no response came, he had tried calling. Xavier had paced the floor until the sun dropped in the sky and he couldn't take worrying any longer. He drove to Dean's shop with his heart in his throat, only to find it closed for the day. That was when the real panic hit.

He drove to Dean's house, trying to beat back the shaking in his gut. Dean had been working so many hours lately that Xavier worried about him driving home so late every night. Had he been in a wreck?

Surely Brett would have said something. Then again, no one had told him when Brett had been in his wreck and Xavier had been living with him at the time. Xavier felt sick. When he got to Dean's house and his knock went unanswered, the feeling doubled. The garage was locked up tight, so Xavier had no way of knowing if Dean's bike was inside. With no other options left to him, he texted Brett.

Xavier: *Have you seen or heard from Dean today?*
Brett: *No. Why?*
Xavier: *I haven't either and I'm getting worried.*
Brett: *Give me a minute.*

While Xavier waited to see if Brett could find out what he could not, Xavier stared at Dean's house from behind the wheel of his SUV. He kind of liked Dean's tiny house. The guy couldn't get away from him when they were under the same roof. Still, Xavier wished they didn't have different roofs sometimes. He didn't think he was ready to move in together or anything like that. It was more of a longing in his gut to avoid moments like these. They were a couple. He shouldn't have to get Brett to track him down. Not knowing where Dean was shouldn't be an issue they had.

Brett: *I texted him. He says he's at The Back Porch.*

Goddamn it. What the fuck was going on? Xavier was relieved as hell that Dean wasn't dead in a ditch somewhere, but why was he ignoring Xavier? Xavier quickly thanked Brett and then broke every speed limit to get to Dean before he could get away. He had to figure out what in the fuck was going on. Xavier didn't understand it. His biggest fear was that Dean had awoken in the middle of the night and thought Xavier had sneaked away. He had, but he had immediately regretted it. Dean wasn't weak, though. If he had thought Xavier had left his bed, he would have confronted him. Right? Fuck. Xavier didn't know any longer, but apparently, he would find out.

DEAN COULDN'T SIT HOME ANY LONGER. THE walls were closing in on him. Every second that passed without a distraction was a second that Dean fought the urge to call Xavier. He hadn't known it was possible to miss a person so much. This was exactly why he hadn't wanted to mess with Xavier in the first place. He had known it would be this way when Xavier tired of him. Fuck. He couldn't keep chasing this same circle inside his mind.

For an hour, Dean rode around town on his bike, enjoying the weather. At one point, he hit the interstate and opened her up, hitting breakneck speeds before moving to the shoreline and slowing down. Nothing brought him peace. Without realizing where he was headed, Dean found himself at The Back Porch. As always, the parking lot was packed. Considering it was Wednesday night, Dean expected it to be a little less busy, but no.

As Dean cleared the door, his steps slowed. The back of the place had been cleared of tables and a stage had been brought in. The room was oddly silent, as if everyone awaited whatever came next. Wrecker headed his way, pulling Dean's attention away from the stage. Dean hadn't seen the owner since he had gotten married. Not that Dean was a frequent patron. Still, Dean had always liked the ex pro football player.

Dean flashed him a smile. "Hey, man. What's up?" He nodded toward the stage, letting Wrecker know his question was directed at the new setup.

Wrecker quickly glanced behind him before focusing on Dean again. "It's a thing we've been doing for a while on Wednesdays. People get to showcase their talents. It's all in good fun. How have you been? I don't think I've seen you around in over a year."

Dean shrugged. "Meh. You know how it is. I have a business to run, so I'm usually doing my thing."

Wrecker nodded. His lion-like eyes always made Dean feel like he saw too much. "Yep, I get that. I've got a table open right here," he said, pointing at a table right next to the door. "Everyone likes to be close to the stage, so it's usually pretty quiet back here. If you want to move closer, I'm sure someone has an open seat at their table."

Dean shook his head. "Back here is fine. I just came for the coffee."

With a nod, Wrecker took a step back. "I'll get on that, then. Enjoy your night."

Dean let his smile slip away as Wrecker left him alone. He wasn't in the mood to fake happiness. Dean dropped his helmet on the table as he sat. He pulled out his phone so he could focus on something other than his surroundings. In truth, He didn't see a thing. Maybe he shouldn't have ordered any coffee. He should just go home. Before Xavier, Dean had been fine while doing nothing by himself. Now everything felt empty. He needed to learn to be alone again. It was just that he had missed a million and one texts and calls from Xavier and Dean felt sick. He wanted to answer, but he just couldn't. Dean couldn't let himself weaken.

A body filled the seat across from him.

Dean's head shot up.

Dawson didn't smile. In fact, he didn't even look Dean's way. He sat sideways in his chair, as if keeping his attention split between the stage and Dean. "So, are you still dating the supermodel?"

Dean snorted. "Does anyone ever really date a supermodel or do they date you until they're done?"

He could tell Dawson smiled by the curve of his cheek. "Probably that second one."

Dean put his phone away. He kind of liked the fact that Dawson wasn't looking at him. Dean didn't feel the need to smile or fake it. He was also free to stare at Dawson without making things awkward. The guy was really gorgeous in a subdued way. Dean had been so struck by Xavier that he hadn't even noticed the chiseled features Dawson kept hidden behind a few days' worth of facial hair. He looked nice.

It hit Dean that he hadn't really answered Dawson's question. "He's done with me."

Dawson turned his head and met Dean's stare.

His light brown eyes seemed a little darker tonight. "Sometimes life just kicks you in the balls."

A genuine smile tugged at the corners of his mouth. "True story." Dean's smile immediately fell. "I'm sorry about the last time we spoke. I had no idea Xavier would show up. We weren't together then and I never would've flirted with you if I had been with him. I'm not that guy."

Someone spoke into the microphone. Dawson glanced over his shoulder. Dean's gaze went to the stage. There was a beautiful man with dark hair standing on stage. He had a dimple in his chin and a soulful air—like everyone leaned forward in their seats, entranced. When he spoke, Dean automatically swallowed. His voice was like being wrapped in a warm blanket. Poetry poured from the man like his soul stripped bare for the room.

"My gaze moves over his skin like a lover's touch. I can't stop. Time and time again, I torture myself with the sight of him. I've never wanted anyone this much. It's unfair for me to feel this way. It's not him. It's me. Isn't that what people say? We are a mistake. At least that's what he says each time I wake."

Dawson turned away from the poet and met Dean's stare. "I'm in love with someone else. Likely I should be the one apologizing." Dean didn't know what to say. Dawson kept talking, saving Dean from having to figure out where to go from that sudden confession. "He paints and writes poetry." A sad smile touched Dawson's lips and Dean fought the urge to glance toward the stage again. In fact, Dean felt his eyes grow bigger as he internally struggled not to look at the poet onstage. Dawson visibly swallowed. "He's insanely talented and creative as hell and we can never, ever be together."

A movement behind Dawson caught Dean's eye. The gorgeous boy from the stage headed their way, sandwiched between Remington and Roscoe. The couple were well known for picking a third to join their bed. It seemed they had snagged the person who owned Dawson's heart the instant he stepped off stage. Dean couldn't tear his gaze from the guy. He looked super young but not innocent. There was a tiny diamond earring in his nose and his eyes were an amazing shade of silver. Dean's heart dropped as the three men left together while Dawson stared unblinking in the opposite direction. He swore he felt the waves of pain crashing over Dawson. They were quite the pair, Dawson and him. Dean had to do something.

He grabbed his helmet. "I think Wrecker forgot my coffee. There's a spare helmet at my shop. Would you like to follow me over there and then go for a ride? We could head to the coast and camp out on the beach. Watch the sunrise. Forget about life."

Dawson's gaze latched on to Dean again. He eyes looked the way Dean felt—like everything beneath his skin was broken and he was one wrong word away from coming apart at the seams. "I think I'd like that."

Dean stood while holding his helmet much tighter than necessary. He knew he grasped at straws to save himself. But maybe, just maybe, he could also save Dawson. It looked like they both needed someone right now. With Xavier gone, Dean had all the time in the world.

For longer than Xavier cared to admit, he sat in his SUV and watched Dean with Dawson. They didn't touch. In fact, they rarely looked each other's way, but still. Dean wasn't answering his calls and was with another man. It was a blow. Xavier wanted to burst inside The Back Porch and become the crazy boyfriend, but something didn't feel right. There was still this niggling feeling in the back of Xavier's mind. He had sneaked away from Dean's bed. Xavier had done that. The guilt was real and colored everything.

Finally, Dean came to his feet. Dawson did too. Xavier's hand gripped the door handle. He had to see where this was headed. Dean stepped outside, followed by Dawson. They said something to each other then parted ways. Dean headed for his bike. Xavier leapt from his vehicle, cutting him off halfway, ready to blast Dean for ignoring him while spending his time with Dawson. They were supposed to be a couple. He thought they were exclusive. Dean's gaze landed on Xavier and Xavier's heart skipped a beat. Dean's eyes looked dead—like he felt nothing for Xavier. Xavier's rage doubled. He had been worrying all day and Dean had the nerve to look at him like this. He had the audacity to be out with Dawson.

"What the fuck, Dean? I've been trying to call you. I thought you were dead in a ditch somewhere until Brett said you were here."

Dean's forehead furrowed. "Why do you care?"

Xavier drew back, feeling slapped. "What the fuck is that supposed to mean? Why wouldn't I care?"

Dean's jaw flexed—like he ground his back teeth. "Why are you here?"

Xavier felt his face screw up in confusion. "Um, because we're a couple and I've been looking for you all goddamn day and you're not answering my calls."

"No, we're not."

The fight drained from Xavier. His confusion doubled. "Did I miss something? I feel like a fight happened that I don't know about. Tell me what I did wrong."

"Oh, Coral, you know I'm boring. I'm not dating anyone," Dean said in a mocking and over-exaggerated accent. "You're not dating anyone, so go away."

Xavier's confusion cleared. He snorted. He couldn't believe all this was because of Coral's show. "Everyone knows you don't tell Coral Jones you're dating anyone unless you plan to marry them. She'll assign you a honeymoon destination before the words stop resounding in the air. Her show is just an hour-long fluff piece. Nobody takes anything serious from there."

Dean's hard expression didn't soften. In fact, Xavier wondered if he should protect his face from an incoming hit. "Did you run all those words through a filter in your head and decide it was the right thing to say right now?"

The confusion was back. He didn't understand

Dean at all. They had only been dating three months and Dean was already hinting to Xavier that he loved him and now he was angry Xavier didn't want Coral setting a wedding date for them. Xavier didn't understand what was happening. He also didn't know the right answer. "Yes," he said, dragging out the word, since he wasn't sure it was the right response.

Dean's eyes fell closed and it hit Xavier. He truly had hurt Dean by denying their relationship on Coral's show. He opened his mouth, intent on explaining or apologizing. Even he didn't know which. Dean focused on him again. He truly looked devastated. The words stuck in Xavier's throat. "I don't think I'm the one for you."

"Don't say that." The laughter in Xavier's voice was pure self-preservation. He didn't like where this was headed, and he had never been good with confrontation. "We're great together."

Dean didn't soften. "Let me rephrase that. You're not the one for me."

Xavier tried to smile to hide the way Dean's claim cut to the bone. "What are you saying?"

"I'm saying, you want to be single in the public's eye, so you can be single in private too. Have a nice life, Xavier."

"Dean—"

Dean stepped around him and straddled his bike, leaving Xavier standing there with his heart in his throat. He didn't understand what he had done wrong. One talk show meant nothing. Seriously, no one took Coral's show to heart. Xavier had never hidden Dean from anyone. They had been to several places together—like...

The air left Xavier's lungs. They never actually went anywhere together, he realized too late. Most of the time, they went from one house to the other. Dean hadn't complained, so Xavier hadn't thought anything of it. He thought they were happy. That was the one thought that kept trying to take out his knees. If Dean had just said something, Xavier would have tried harder. He never dreamed keeping them shielded from Coral's meddling ways would lead to exposing so many cracks in something he had considered flawless. As he watched Dean ride away, the horrible sensations in his chest and gut that he had barely held at bay all day finally swept him under. He couldn't make his legs work to walk back to his car. Xavier didn't understand how they could be over. He didn't understand anything anymore. They had been happy. He was sure of it.

SIX

DEAN STARED AT A VASE FILLED WITH multicolored roses while chewing on his bottom lip. He turned the vase from side to side. The card on the counter next to the flowers mocked Dean with a life he could never have. Another Xavier apology. The thing was, a few weeks apart had given Dean clarity. They had been a beautiful illusion and nothing more. Dean hadn't realized Xavier had been hiding them. He thought Xavier—like him—simply enjoyed a quiet life of being at home. It never once occurred to him that Xavier was ashamed. Not once. Then they had split, and Dean saw things as they were. Xavier never wanted to go in public, claiming he would get mobbed. It hadn't once crossed Dean's mind he was being hidden. What a fool he had been.

Just a great big dumbass happy to have some famous dude's attention. Now he kept getting these damn flowers and he no longer knew what to believe, but he knew one thing with absolute certainty. He had been much happier in their relationship than Xavier had been. Dean wouldn't steal any more of the man's time and he absolutely would not keep him from Sweden.

"More flowers from Xavier?"

Dean glanced up as Dawson strolled through the door of his shop. "Yeah. I hate to keep throwing them away, but they're wasted on me." A smile lit Dean's face as an idea struck. "You should leave them on Milo's doorstep with no card."

A sardonic-looking smile touched Dawson's lips. "You should keep them. Money means nothing to someone like Xavier and you deserve nice things."

Dean turned the vase again, enjoying the changing of colors from red to pink. "Do men like getting flowers?"

A chuckle rumbled from Dawson's chest. "You're a man. Do you like getting flowers?"

"I'm undecided," Dean answered, turning the vase again. "That's why I asked."

Dawson leaned his elbows on the counter and eyed the roses. "I'm not sure I'm the person to ask.

Before Milo, I didn't really see the beauty in anything."

Dawson's expression had a sad smile tugging at Dean's lips. "You should see your face right now."

While clearing his throat, Dawson straightened away from the counter and turned his back on Dean. He wandered over to the sketches on the wall, eyeing them as he spoke. "You do amazing work. Are you willing to do tattoos of images other people bring in?"

Dean let the change in subject stand. He was too tired of his broken heart to keep talking about anything heavy. "Of course."

Dawson pulled a sliver of paper out of his pocket as he moved back to the counter. "What about this? Could you match the handwriting?"

"This was a mistake," Dean read aloud.

A bright smile lit Dawson's face. It was completely fake. "I want it on my chest—like a joke. You know, this was a mistake."

Dean forced a laugh he didn't feel. He recognized a final note when he saw one. To hide his true reaction, Dean turned away and flattened the note on his scanner. The paper had seen better days —like it was old and someone had carried it around in their pocket for years. "If you're serious, I'll print this out onto transfer paper so I can trace the handwriting. That way, it'll be perfect."

"Yeah, I'm totally serious. You're my friend. There's no one else I'd trust to handle my first tattoo."

That had Dean facing Dawson again. "Are you serious? I get to be your first?"

Dawson's bright smile was irresistible. "Yep. You're taking my ink virginity."

"I promise to be gentle," Dean said with a wink.

"Are you just sticking in the tip?"

A burst of laughter escaped Dean. It turned into a roar. He found himself swiping at his eyes, trying to catch his breath. It felt like it had been so long since he laughed.

"You don't laugh enough. You have a great laugh."

Unexpectedly, Dean's throat swelled. A wave of longing washed over him. He missed Xavier. No one had ever made him laugh as much as the outrageous and over-the-top arrogant ass he had fallen in love with. Dean took a breath and tried to cling to the moment of happiness he had found by just being with his friend. He pushed Xavier from his mind.

"I'll try harder if you do."

Dawson gave him a sharp nod. "It's a deal. I'll do

my best to keep you smiling and laughing until you're back with Xavier."

Dean snorted. "I guess you're investing forever in me, then. Xavier and I are done."

Dawson's gaze slid in the roses' direction and stayed. "I disagree, and I think these flowers do too." He moved closer to the vase and picked up the card sitting next to it. Dawson read the words aloud while Dean stood paralyzed with a love that had nowhere to go anymore. "Dean, I know flowers are cliché, but I still think you deserve them. I know apologizing isn't enough. Please let me try to make things right between us. I miss you more than words can say. Please call me, X." Dawson set the card aside. He didn't meet Dean's stare. "Wow. It sounds like he's sorry. Do you really have no plans to forgive him for one mistake? Your love is pretty thin, if that's the case."

A shot of outrage rang through Dean at the accusation. It died as quickly as it flared to life. "There's more to it than him claiming to be single in front of the whole world, even though that's pretty damn huge." Dean swallowed. He wanted to say that he couldn't be the reason someone else lost their parents. Dean needed to talk about how his selfishness had already cost Brett and him their parents, so he couldn't keep Xavier here in the US and away from his. The thing was, though, he had never been able to shape those words. Dean had never been able to express how the guilt kept him up at night and weighed on his soul. He couldn't talk about how he hadn't let his brother buy him a house in a nice neighborhood. Dean damn sure couldn't talk about how Xavier wanting to move back to Sweden was bigger than all the relationship denials in the world.

Instead of saying the things he probably should, Dean motioned toward a side room he used to keep patrons' privacy while he worked. "Let's get started."

Dawson shook his head, as if giving up, and headed inside the room. Dean followed on his heels, determined to let Xavier go. He felt certain he was meant to be alone. After all, life kept stealing everyone from him. Soon his brother would be married, and Dean would be just someone Brett saw on holidays. The only person Dean really had was himself. He needed to watch out for his heart first from now on. Dean quickly reversed course. He grabbed the vase and tossed it in the trash. It was time to leave Xavier in the past. They had to go their separate ways. That was best for everyone. Xavier could return to Sweden guilt free. Dean could... He didn't know. Grow old and fade away, he supposed. It didn't matter. Xavier was free now. Dean had gotten a moment of beauty with him. He should have never expected more.

XAVIER STOOD OUTSIDE THE MAD TATTER WITH his heart in his throat. He had been there for several minutes, trying to talk himself into going inside. Except Dawson was inside with Dean and then Dean had thrown Xavier's flowers away. Xavier turned away. He supposed he should go home. Dean didn't want him anymore.

Somewhere along the drive, Xavier lost sight of his destination and ended up parked in Brett's driveway. He sat so long, trying to decide why he had come here instead of going home, Roman came outside to meet him.

He opened up Xavier's driver's side door. "Things are that bad, huh?"

"Yep." Xavier couldn't even look Roman's way.

Roman made a humming sound—like thinking things through. "Tell me what you've tried so far."

"Lots of flowers and notes. Several food

deliveries so he doesn't go hungry. Countless calls and texts." Even to Xavier's ears, he sounded dead.

"Did any of those notes and texts include an apology?"

Xavier's hands rose and fell, because he had nothing. "All of them. Be honest with me. Am I that bad of a person? What did I do that was so unfixable?"

Roman took a step back and shook his head. "You're my friend and you're not going to like what I have to say about this, so don't ask."

Xavier bit back a growl. "You're right. We're friends. That's why I'm asking. I know you'll be honest."

Roman tilted his chin to the sky as if seeking guidance from above. After a second passed, he blew out a sigh and focused on Xavier. "Fine. I think things come to you too easily and Dean is the opposite. Everyone wants to be near you because of who you are. Dean has a hard time making friends and maybe I shouldn't have urged you to pursue this relationship."

"What's that supposed to mean?" Even Xavier heard the anger in his voice.

"See," Roman said, sounding exasperated. "This is exactly why I didn't want to have this conversation. You're getting upset and I don't want that."

Xavier barely stopped himself from stamping his feet like a child. He was so frustrated with everything, he didn't know where to go with it. "I'm upset because Dean broke up with me and I don't really understand what I did wrong. Everyone knows Coral's show isn't to be taken seriously. Hers isn't the place to be telling the world about a special relationship. I don't understand."

Roman's expression cleared. He focused on Xavier like everything inside him had gone still. "You really don't understand what you did wrong," Roman repeated—like he couldn't believe his ears. "I'm not in your relationship, and even I know what you did wrong." Roman sounded so outraged that Xavier was speechless. All he could do was listen, since Roman wasn't finished. "I haven't talked to him to hear his side of the story, and still I know what you did. You went on a live nationwide show and told the entire world you were single. You didn't think that would cut someone like him to the bone? Damn, Xavier. You couldn't have possibly denied being with him any more publicly than that. Even I felt like I had been stabbed in the heart when I watched you say those words and it had nothing to do with me. Fuck, Xavier. Have you not noticed that Dean has no one other than his brother? His own parents don't want him anymore. You're supposed to be the one person who wants him whether it's at a fluff show no one cares about or in the middle of The Back Porch. You're supposed to be proud to be with him. Especially since you're the first man he's ever dated, yet he didn't deny being with you to anyone. Damn what the world thought about him suddenly dating a man, Dean didn't hide you. What you did was fucked up, man. For real, it was a shitty thing to do. If you don't get that, I don't know how to make you understand. Maybe just think about how you would feel if he had been the one who told everyone you two weren't dating—like he was embarrassed to be with you."

"I'm not embarrassed to be with him." Xavier had never been so frustrated in his life.

A sad look passed over Roman's face. "Well, good luck proving that to him now that your actions said otherwise."

"Damn, Roman. I want to prove it to him, but he won't talk to me."

Roman spent a moment staring at Xavier, as if mulling over Xavier's problem. After a minute, he shrugged. "He'll be at the wedding this weekend. That's not something he can skip."

That was true. They would both be at the wedding, but Xavier would have to skate a thin line. He couldn't ruin Roman's wedding, but he had to get Dean alone. Xavier needed a plan.

Roman patted his shoulder. "Why don't you try texting him about something other than your breakup? He probably needs a break from the anger and hurt as much as you do. You should remind him that you used to be happy together."

Xavier nodded, even though he didn't think he would follow Roman's advice. It was possible they were truly done for good. Maybe the fact that one moment of stupidity could ruin them was all the truth he needed. They hadn't been as strong as he thought. Possibly Dean was better off without him. Xavier had never been that great of a person. He should go back to what he did best. Being a self-absorbed bastard. Maybe tomorrow he would send himself flowers and fuck going to Roman's wedding this weekend. He had been alone before Dean. He could go back to that again. Yes. That was what he would do.

He flashed Roman a smile he didn't feel. "Thanks for being my friend."

Roman's expression snapped closed—like Xavier's tone made him suspicious. "What are you about to do?"

Xavier took a deep breath, letting the hurt settle into his bones. "I'm going home." Back to his solitude. "Things have been crazy and awful, so—in case I haven't said so already—I'm really happy for you and I hope everything goes great this weekend."

"Why do you sound like you're not coming?"

Xavier's smile turned faker by the second. "Everything is fine. Don't worry over me."

Even though Roman didn't look convinced, he took a step back and closed Xavier's door. Xavier needed to go home. It was well past the time for him to get back to reality. Back to his life. He had become too dependent on Brett and then Dean, feeling like a part of their family with his so far away. That was over. They weren't his family. Xavier needed to remember that. He needed to let them go.

WITH THE SHOP CLOSED AND DAWSON GONE, Dean stared at nothing and soaked up the silence. His gaze moved to the expensive hydraulic tattoo table he had bought for the business before he opened. It had served him well. Dean planned to buy another as soon as he could spare the funds. A smile tugged at the corners of his mouth. No one would touch the thing if they knew what Xavier had done to him on it after closing one night. Dean fought a blush. Xavier had stripped him bare, spread him wide, and taught Dean all about what it was like to get finger fucked. Xavier had massaged places Dean hadn't known existed, dragging orgasm after orgasm from Dean. It had been one hell of a night.

Even as Dean's heart ached, his cock stirred. He reached down and adjusted himself. Before he could stop it from happening, Dean found himself scrolling through his phone and reading their old texts from back when they had been happy. Dean had never missed anyone so much in his life. He didn't know how to stop. Dean craved the sound of Xavier's heart beating against his ear. He missed the sensation of Xavier's nude body against his. As much as he liked Dawson and as happy as he was for Dawson's friendship right now, no one could possibly understand. He had gone from what he thought was this beautiful and perfect relationship to nothing overnight. The loss was too hard to swallow almost every second of the day.

Suddenly, as Dean scrolled, his phone jumped to

the bottom of their texts. Three dots appeared, showing Xavier was typing. A small part of him wanted to block the man's number before his text could come in. Dean couldn't do it. Instead, he patiently waited, needing to know what Xavier would say. He fully expected another empty apology. Instead, Xavier surprised him.

Xavier: *I made Cavatelli and Mussels again tonight. The first meal we ever shared alone. Now I'm sitting here, dying of curiosity while wondering what you are doing. Have you eaten? Are you getting enough sleep? I drive myself crazy with these questions. I know you won't answer. You never do.*

For a long moment, Dean fought himself. The internal battle was real. He knew he shouldn't respond. Still his fingers typed.

Dean: *I ordered pizza from that place on Maple. It took them two hours to deliver and it was cold by the time it arrived. Since it didn't come on time, I had an appointment anyhow. So I shoved it in the fridge and forgot to eat. At this point, I think I'll just save it for breakfast.*

So much time passed after he sent his text without a response that Dean almost put his phone away when the three dots danced again.

Xavier: *I was waiting for you to answer my*

question about you sleeping, but I guess I've probably gotten all I'll get.

Dean: *You know I don't sleep well when I'm cold. That's why I always snuggled so close to you every night. Well, one of the reasons. I wish I had known you have a sensory disorder. If so, I would've given you your space. I guess I did a lot of things wrong that drove you away when I wasn't looking.*

After hitting send, Dean berated himself. He shouldn't be responding to Xavier's texts, much less whining about their breakup. He quickly tried taking everything back.

Dean: *I wish texting had an unsend option.*

Xavier: *I wish life had an undo button.*

The burning sensation behind his eyes got to be too much. Dean bent over in his seat and pressed his forehead to the edge of the tattoo table where Xavier once made love to him. Everything felt empty and pointless. Dean's phone vibrated again. He focused on the device with his head still resting on the table.

Xavier: *There's enough remorse to go around. I'd rather talk about what I don't regret. I never told you about my hatred of different materials touching my skin because I loved holding you. What are you doing right now?*

Dean: *Sitting inside my closed shop.*

Xavier: *How close are you to the table I love?*

In a moment of weakness, Dean held out his phone and snapped a quick selfie where he was—with his head pressed to the table.

Xavier: *You look sad.*

For a moment, Dean couldn't make his fingers work to respond. Sad was a vast understatement. Dean had never been more miserable in his life.

Dean: *What are you doing right now?*

A picture appeared on Dean's phone. Xavier was in bed, snuggled down in his ridiculous fluffy pillows. Dean hurt all the way to his soul.

Dean: *You look tired. I should let you get some sleep.*

Xavier: *Thank you for talking to me.*

Dean set his phone aside. He couldn't take any more tonight. Instead, he found himself stroking the table and staring at nothing. The nights were the worst. He never wanted to go home anymore. Things just seemed to get darker all the time—like there was no hope left. He would stand at Brett's side this weekend and watch him marry. Dean couldn't think of anything more depressing. He hated everything. Maybe he would give up making a go of this shop and walk away from everything. He could jump on his bike and travel the country. There was nothing keeping him here, except that all he had ever wanted was a steady home and security. Dean just didn't think that life was meant for him unless he wanted to live it alone. Maybe he would become a hermit instead. He could sell the shop, shut down his phone, and buy some small place in the middle of nowhere. No one would miss him. He could just be still and lick his wounds. Maybe that was what he would do. He would think about it until this weekend. Once he saw Brett settled, he would decide his next move. For now, he just wanted to rest right here and remember a wonderful night he had spent with the man of his dreams. Dean would never have those nights back, but they had happened. No one could take the memories away. Those were his. Dean wouldn't forget.

SEVEN

At five minutes until the start of Brett and Roman's wedding, Xavier decided he wouldn't be able to live with himself if he missed their big day. He threw his clothes on as he headed for the door and practically ran next door to Brett's for the wedding. He slid into a chair in the back row just as the music began to play. His gaze latched on to where Dean stood at the front of the transformed party room. In a tux, he waited for the grooms to come down the aisle together. He looked sexy and Xavier wanted to pet him. The ache in Xavier's chest was a level of longing he had never experienced before. His eyes itched as he refused to blink against the sight of Dean. The ceremony began and Xavier didn't hear a word. He couldn't take his eyes off Dean. A time or two, he swore Dean's face turned his way. He tortured himself with the sight of Dean until the very last moment. The second the ceremony ended, and he was free to stand, Xavier headed for a set of French doors closest to the gate that separated their properties. He could say he came. Xavier could live with knowing he hadn't missed his friends' wedding. It wasn't necessary for him to attend the rest of the event.

He almost made his escape.

Dean stepped outside right behind him. "Why are you leaving? I thought Brett and Roman were your friends? Are they not good enough for you either? Do you plan to deny lowering yourself enough to come to their wedding?"

Xavier turned and swiped his hand over his eyes. He was tired of the anger. Xavier had thought they were past this. "Please stop. You know damn well I wasn't embarrassed to be with you. I don't know what else I can do or say to make you understand that."

Dean visibly swallowed—like his throat hurt. "Maybe so, but it doesn't change the fact that I was a lot happier being with you than you were being with me. I get it. You're you and I'm me, but you have to stop teasing me with a life I can't have. A life you don't want."

Frustration choked Xavier. He didn't know how to make Dean understand he didn't want to fight anymore. Xavier was tired of saying he was sorry, only to have it fall on deaf ears. He just wanted things to be the way they used to be, but he knew he couldn't have that. "You're the one who chased me outside. I was trying to leave."

Dawson stepped outside, stopping Xavier from apologizing again for what he couldn't change. "You should come back inside with your brother, Dean. This is his big day."

Xavier snapped. He couldn't stop it from happening. He was so fucking sick of everything. His anger had nowhere to go. "I can't fucking believe how ridiculous this entire situation is. We were fine, Dean. I thought we were happy. One night we were falling asleep together and now you're here with this guy." He pointed at Dawson with all the rage in his heart. "For fuck's sake. He's in love with his brother."

"Milo is not my brother." Dawson's voice shook with outrage. "Goddamn. It's because of people like you we can't be together."

Xavier held his hands up in surrender, really losing his shit. He couldn't believe Dean had brought fucking Dawson with him as his date. "Excuse the hell out of me. Your *foster* brother, but don't you dare blame me for you being a pussy. The two of you not being together is no one's fault but your own. Everyone on the entire goddamn planet knows Milo is always at The Back Porch, doing everything he can to get your attention, yet you're here with the man I love. Every time I turn around, you're with the man I love. Jesus. Go be with your man so I can have five goddamn minutes alone with mine." Xavier was yelling at the top of his lungs, but he couldn't stop. He was furious with life.

"You love me?"

The quietly spoken question pulled Xavier from his rage. His gaze locked on to Dean's hope-filled face and the anger melted away. He just wanted to be with Dean. He couldn't express that deeply enough. "Of course I love you. If you would answer my calls or sit still for five seconds, I would tell you how much I love everything about you. Do you think I've ever chased anyone or called anyone nonstop after getting dumped before you? Why would I do that for someone I don't love?"

A hint of a smile touched Dean's lips.

"Honestly? I doubt you've ever been dumped."

Despite the situation, a smile tugged at the corners of Xavier's mouth. "Not true. I've had my heart broken." His smile slipped. "By you."

Dean shook his head. His eyes fell closed. He looked like he tried to shake off Xavier's spell. "No. You said you wanted to move back to Sweden to be near your parents. I can't do this."

Xavier's forehead furrowed. He looked Dawson's way to see if he understood that statement. Dawson was gone, leaving Xavier to puzzle things out by himself. "What in the hell are you talking about?"

"On Coral's show," Dean explained. "You said you hoped to move back to Sweden, so pursuing this would be a waste of both our time. I can't leave Brett. He wouldn't leave me, and I've already caused Brett to lose our parents by him choosing me. You can't choose me."

Xavier shook his head. He couldn't believe the words leaving Dean's mouth. Surely Dean didn't really believe any of that. Xavier moved closer and rubbed Dean's arms. Dean let it happen, so Xavier didn't stop. It felt like forever since they last touched. "Sweetie, no. Good parents don't stop talking to their children because they want a better life. Good parents love you no matter how many miles stand between you. You can't make good parents stop talking to their children. Your parents stopped talking to Brett and you because they're pieces of shit and Brett hasn't done you any favors by not saying that to you before now."

Dean shook his head again. "It doesn't matter. You want to move back to Sweden. I don't want that. You're wasting your time with me."

Xavier laughed. He couldn't help it. Xavier kind of loved the fact that Dean thought life was black and white. That he still thought the world was a huge place. "Sweetie. You do realize that I have enough money to live here and there, right? Like we could have visited Sweden for a month in the summer and two in the winter if you had given me a chance." He felt Dean's muscles relax beneath his hands where he still held Dean's arms. Xavier kept talking, breaking down the walls Dean had built between them. "Not to mention, my mom loves L.A. I wouldn't be surprised if she decided to move here in the next few years, especially since my younger brother already intends to move here next year. You know that I'm an actor. My job is here. I don't have any plans of retiring until I'm too old to walk. Your being here, that's only icing for me. I love you and I don't want to be with anyone else, but you're not stealing me from anyone. I chose this place long before you chose me." He froze as he realized what he said. Xavier swallowed. His eyes burned. "Back when you chose me, that is." Xavier took a step back, setting Dean free. "Dawson is right. You should go back inside. It's your brother's big day."

"What about you? Will you come back inside?"

Xavier shook his head and looked away. "I should've considered... never mind. This is your family. I shouldn't have come in the first place. You have a date waiting for you." Despite his best efforts, Xavier focused on Dean again. He was just too beautiful in Xavier's eyes to ignore. "Have a nice life, gorgeous. I won't bother you anymore." Without looking back, Xavier walked away. It was the right thing to do. He loved Dean, but Dean didn't feel secure with him. Xavier really hoped Dean didn't end up with Dawson, though. Dawson loved someone else and Dean deserved someone whose life revolved around him. Xavier wanted the job, but that wasn't enough. He had learned too late that Dean also needed someone to make him feel rooted and safe. All Xavier had ever seen was the strong side of Dean. He hadn't realized how much Dean needed him to be the strong one until it was too late. So someone else would have to take the job. Xavier rubbed his chest. He hoped they were kind and gave Dean a good life. Xavier would never know. It was time for him to move on.

DEAN WATCHED XAVIER WALK AWAY WITH HIS heart in his throat. His mind screamed for him to chase Xavier down and drag him back inside. But it was his brother's special day. Dean headed back inside. He made a half-assed effort to find Dawson before giving up and taking his seat at Brett's side for dinner. Dean smiled for pictures and made a toast. He laughed as Brett smashed cake in Roman's face. It wasn't until he watched them take the floor for their first dance that the real sadness set in. Xavier had said he loved Dean. It was odd. If anyone had told him that Xavier's love would be enough to wipe away the hurt and anger, Dean would have laughed his ass off. But Xavier's love was enough. Dean wanted it. In fact, he wanted Xavier's affection above and beyond anything else in the world, so he had no idea why he still sat there without him.

Dean snagged a full bottle of champagne and two glasses. He didn't look back as he headed out the same French doors Xavier had left through earlier that evening. There was a gate between Brett's backyard and Xavier's. Dean found it and slipped through. Xavier's backyard always took Dean's breath. It was especially beautiful at night. Sand and palm trees surrounded a man-made beach. The pool lights shimmered, making the water seem extra blue while an island in the center twinkled with tiny bulbs around a tiki hut style cabana. Some expert pool designer had turned Xavier's backyard into a man-made tropical getaway. It was Dean's favorite part of Xavier's home. He made it halfway through the backyard.

"Did you get bored with the dancing?"

Dean's gaze shot to the cabana in the center of the pool. Xavier sat in the middle of a huge lounge chair wearing nothing more than a pair of tiny shorts. Dean fought an inner sigh, trying not to let it out. He loved Xavier's body. "No. I didn't have anyone to dance with, so that makes it kind of hard to get bored with it. Is it okay if I join you?"

Xavier scooted over, making room for Dean. He patted the empty side of the lounge. "Please."

Dean crossed the sand bridge to the island. He held up the champagne as he neared. "I stole us something to drink on my way out." Dean passed the bottle and glasses to Xavier and kicked out of his shoes. He didn't stop there. Dean hated tuxedos. He hated being uncomfortable and hot. Dean stripped off his jacket and started unbuttoning his shirt. "I don't know how you do it. I don't have any sensory issues and I'm ready to scream. These clothes have to go. I'm pissed off because everything feels itchy against my skin." Dean tossed the upper half of his clothes aside. His hands went to the button on his pants. "I can't tolerate another second of this suit."

A wicked-looking smile touched Xavier's lips. "You'll get no complaints from me. While I think you're sexy as hell in that getup, you're so much better in nothing at all."

Dean smiled as he stripped down to nothing but his underwear. He realized, even though they weren't a couple any longer, Dean was still a good ten times happier just being in Xavier's presence. It had always been this way, even before they had dated. Xavier made him better. Dean liked being with him.

He climbed onto the lounge with Xavier. "I don't know anything about champagne, but I know my brother. He bought the best. It's not bad."

Xavier didn't look at the bottle. His gaze never wavered from Dean. "I'm sure. Is the reception winding down?"

Dean shrugged as he popped the cork on the bottle. "I have a feeling that's a party that'll go all night." He poured each of them a glass before setting the bottle aside. "But I've had all the loving glances and overwhelming happiness I can stand for one night." He looked Xavier's way.

Xavier's heated stare took his breath. "Have you really?"

A laugh unexpectedly burst from Dean. "I don't know." They both downed their champagne like Dean's admission had been a toast. Since it was nowhere near the first glass of alcohol he had consumed for the night, the confessions kept coming. "I'm sorry I'm crazy and needy and rushed you to be more than you were ready to be. Above all, you were my friend and I miss that. I'm sorry I demanded too much."

"You'll have to refill my glass if you're determined to make me wade through that complete horse shit."

In his shock, Dean simply passed the bottle Xavier's way without responding.

Xavier set his glass on the ground and turned up the bottle, swallowing several inches before setting the bottle next to his glass. "Okay." He focused on

Dean. "Did you not hear me earlier when I said that I love you?"

"I love you too," Dean said rather than answering.

Xavier's features softened. "Then please stop being angry with me. I shouldn't have said I was still single on Coral's show. Honestly, I didn't do it because I was ashamed, or I didn't want people to know I was taken. I just really didn't want to share you with anyone. You don't realize it, but as soon as people know about you, your life will change. People will take your picture everywhere you go. You'll never have another minute of peace. I didn't want to do that to you before we had a real conversation about it. I didn't want to lose you by scaring you away with the reality of being with me. We fit so well and managed to keep things peaceful and real in a way I've never gotten to experience with anyone before. It was like we were a normal couple. I've never had that. Everyone I've ever dated was out there for public consumption. You were different. I loved that we were different." Xavier's eyes looked sad. "But I should have thought about how you felt. I should've done more to make you feel secure in what we had. I'm sorry that I didn't know I was failing us by being selfish and keeping you to myself."

Dean fought a growl. He no longer knew who was wrong or if anyone was right. "Please stop apologizing. You've said you're sorry so many times that it does nothing but piss me off. Fuck. Can't we just be still and be together for a minute?"

"Let me do something first and then I'll let it go. I promise."

Dean nodded.

Xavier picked something up and leaned his way. Before Dean knew it would happen, Xavier pressed his lips to Dean's ear, making a loud smacking sound that had a smile stretching his lips. Xavier snapped a selfie of them and then settled down beside him. He clicked around on his phone for a minute. "There." He handed the device Dean's way.

Dean stared at the image of them. He looked so happy with Xavier kissing him. His smile stretched from ear to ear. He had one eye closed, visibly struggling against the loud kissing noise. It was the sweetest and goofiest picture. After a moment of staring at it, Dean realized it was an Instagram post. He read the caption. "I love this man more than anything. He makes me happier than I've ever been in my life." Dean's gaze snapped to Xavier's face.

Xavier shrugged. "If you want me to delete it, I can."

Dean set the phone aside and out of Xavier's reach. He shook his head. "I'd like to try to make you happy again, if you'll let me."

"You're here. I'm happy."

Xavier sounded genuine. Hope flared to life inside Dean for the first time since that stupid morning show. "Does that mean you'll be my boyfriend again?"

An adorable smile lit Xavier's face. "I'm pretty sure I never stopped. I've just been waiting for you to come back." Xavier's smile slipped. "I'm fighting the urge to say I'm sorry again."

"Why don't you kiss me instead?"

Happiness filled Dean to completion as Xavier scrambled onto his knees. He straddled Dean's lap and captured his lips. The breath stuttered from Dean's lungs as their tongues met and stroked. He had thought he wouldn't get to taste Xavier again. Dean silently swore he wouldn't take a single second for granted. Xavier was everything to him. He wouldn't let this go again.

Xavier couldn't believe Dean was there. They kissed like they hadn't seen each other in months rather than weeks. The mixture of relief and happiness Xavier experienced while his tongue stroked Dean's was immeasurable. "Don't stop talking to me again," Xavier begged as he changed angles. His eyes burned. The silence had been the worst part. He hadn't known life could feel so empty until Dean brought happiness into his home and then stole it away.

"I'm not. We're fine. I swear." Dean stroked Xavier's back and massaged his ass, hauling him closer. "You're mine. I can't give you up."

Xavier nodded. He would accept Dean's promise. "From now on, we talk to each other or fight it out. No more walking away. You're my best friend. I can't lose you."

Dean held Xavier's face between his hands, forcing Xavier to hold his stare. His gaze moved over Xavier's face—like he searched for any sign Xavier lied. His mouth lifted in one corner into a sexy smirk. "You're my best friend too. Why are you wearing shorts? I thought you didn't like clothes against your skin?"

Xavier drew back in mock horror. "Oh dear. Are you trying to get me out of my clothes already?"

Somehow, Dean's expression turned even more wicked. "I'm just concerned about your health."

A roar of laughter burst from Xavier. He had missed Dean more than words could say. Xavier snuggled as close as he could get and buried his face in the crook of Dean's neck. Dean smelled good. Xavier's lips automatically brushed the spot beneath Dean's ear. "Damn. I love you."

Dean wrapped his arms around Xavier and squeezed. "I love you too. Do you think we could just go to bed and snuggle and refuse to budge for a few days? I didn't know it was possible to miss someone so much. I don't want to let go."

Xavier slipped from Dean's lap and stood. He held his hand out. "Come on."

Dean stood and linked fingers with Xavier, seemingly uncaring of anything except being with Xavier. Hand in hand, they headed for the outdoor shower at Xavier's back door to wash away any sand before going inside. As the warm water washed over Xavier, Dean attacked. Xavier found himself backed against the imitation rock wall that hid the shower heads as Dean's mouth covered his. Dean shoved at Xavier's shorts, stripping him bare. Xavier wasted no time, doing the same, and stealing Dean's underwear. As their mouths clashed, they each tried pulling the other closer. Xavier fought for air as Dean's wet body moved against him, making him painfully aroused.

Dean had always turned him on unlike anyone else. He wasn't fake like everyone else in L.A. Dean's open desire for Xavier was one hundred percent genuine and that was sexier than all the body building and surgically perfected men in the world. Xavier had missed the hair on Dean's chest, his soft belly, and the way he smelled. He had missed everything.

"I've barely slept from craving you," Dean said, mirroring Xavier's thoughts. He reached between them and held their cocks together to stroke. "All I've done is stare at your empty side of the bed every night, longing for your weight in my arms."

The wall was the only thing keeping Xavier upright. Between the pleasure and Dean's confessions, his knees no longer worked.

Dean wasn't finished. He teased Xavier's body and mind with everything he craved. "All I could think about was how long and empty life would be without you. My arms and body felt useless without you. My heart and soul constantly screamed out for their other half. I'm not whole without you."

Xavier had never wanted anyone inside him as badly in his life, but he knew he would never make it inside to the lube and condoms. He needed what Dean currently gave him more than anything else:

validation. They were real. This relationship was the forever kind. Xavier ran his hands up Dean's chest and thrust, fucking Dean's fist and savoring the sensation of his dick against Dean's. Dean's lips parted. His eyes turned unfocused, as if the ecstasy stole his full attention. That thought made him feel powerful. Xavier rooted his feet and thrust again, using his muscle control to take charge.

"Fuck." Dean's breathless curse added to Xavier's determination. There was no position that stopped Xavier from pleasing Dean.

"That's it, my heart. Tighten your grip. Feel my cock moving against yours. Let the pressure build." As Xavier spoke, he was the one who felt the pressure building. Orgasm beat at his crown, ready to blow from just the sensation of Dean's erection against his. "Give me your cum, Dean. Let this first one fly so I can take you inside and finger your asshole. Let me spend the night showing you how much pleasure I can squeeze from you before you can't get it up anymore. Then I'll prove you can orgasm without ever getting hard."

"Oh god." Dean's harsh whisper sounded lost—like he was too close to stop the oncoming tide.

Xavier strained against Dean's palm and cock. He ground his back teeth, reaching for release. "Give it to me," Xavier growled, needing Dean's hot cum on his skin. When the first drop of Dean's cum hit Xavier's crown, an orgasm ripped from Xavier. A cry tore from his throat. He rode the waves while whimpering through each one. Dean's mouth covered his. Xavier bit at Dean's lips until the madness faded and their kiss turned sweet.

"I love you," Dean whispered against his lips, causing Xavier to blink back tears. He had never been so overcome. This was the man he had waited his entire life to meet. Xavier wouldn't lose him again.

"I love you too. Please don't ever give up on me again. I didn't think I would make it without you."

Dean squeezed Xavier to his chest. "I'm not going anywhere. You're mine and I'm pretty sure you completely own me. I don't want a life without you in it."

Xavier held on, soaking up Dean's love as he gently rocked Xavier from side to side. With his eyes squeezed shut, Xavier let their affection seep into his skin and take control of his heart. He couldn't wrap his arms around Dean tightly enough. Xavier never wanted to move from this spot. He was home in more ways than one. Now Xavier just had to find a way to convince Dean to call this place home too, because they were never sleeping apart again. Xavier's mind was set. He had already lost Dean once. Never again. He would find a way.

EIGHT

Since Dean had planned to stay the night at Brett's after the wedding, he had clothes in his old bedroom waiting. Dean just wished he had the foresight to bring them with him to Xavier's. Then he wouldn't have been forced to make the walk of shame from Xavier's place to Brett's while wearing Xavier's workout shorts, and with Xavier following on his heels, smiling like the idiot he was.

"Everyone's going to know you got lucky last night," Xavier said in a sing-song voice behind him.

Dean wanted to be irritated, but he was too happy. "Shut up." Even Dean heard the laughter in his voice. Luckily, they made it to Dean's room without running into anyone along the way.

Xavier crowded Dean's space as they crossed the

threshold into Dean's teenage bedroom. "Come on. I want to see all the things. Do you have pictures of women with big boobs on the walls?"

Dean snorted.

Xavier turned in a circle, eyeing the bare walls. "Well. That's disappointing."

Dean tossed his sand-filled and limp tux on the dresser. "You used to live here. Didn't you explore the house when you were staying with Brett?"

Xavier shook his head. "Not really. He assigned me a bedroom near the kitchen, and I stayed in my own space. It seemed rude to snoop."

Dean closed the door, shutting them inside. "Yet, as I recall, you always walked around nude. That wasn't rude, but snooping is?"

"You know I have my reasons for always being nude." The huff in Xavier's voice couldn't be missed.

Even though Dean knew Xavier's hurt was feigned, he couldn't resist him. He closed the distance between them. "Oh, baby. I know." Dean brushed his fingers through Xavier's hair. "Feel free to poke through all my things now. I took most everything with me when I moved out, but you might find one or two things."

With a wink, Xavier turned away and plopped

down on the bed. "Nope. I'm here for the show. Get to stripping, sexy."

"I'm just changing clothes so we can go to The Back Porch. You've been well fed." Dean tried sounding firm.

"I know." Xavier's leer said he didn't know a damn thing. Dean's cock stirred. Fuck. It wasn't fair for any one person to be so sexual.

Dean didn't move.

Xavier's eyebrows rose. "I thought you were changing so we could go."

"I'm afraid."

At Dean's admission, Xavier's expression shifted. A line appeared between his eyebrows. "What's wrong, baby?"

"If I move, I'm going to get hard. You look too sexy on that bed."

Xavier stood. "Let me help, gorgeous. It'll be okay." Xavier reached for Dean's shorts.

A laugh burst from Dean. "No. That's not helping. What are you doing?"

"I'm helping. I'm a good helper. You'll see."

Dean covered his face with both hands as Xavier peeled off his shorts. Just as he feared, he was rock hard. A hot suction surrounded his cock. Dean dropped his hands and his chin. Xavier was on his knees. Dean stroked Xavier's face while Xavier swallowed his dick. "Why are you like this? This is why we never make it out of the house."

Xavier pulled away but kept pumping Dean's erection. "I suggest you come quick, then. I want coffee."

Dean was stupid in love with this over-the-top guy. He also needed to make sure his baby got some coffee. "Fine. Get to work, then." Dean tugged Xavier's hair, leading him back to his dick. He rolled his hips and openly fucked Xavier's mouth, savoring every wet pull on his cock. His eyes tried rolling back in his head as Xavier squeezed his balls and fingered his asshole. Xavier always got results. In no time, Dean's entire body jerked as he filled Xavier's mouth full of cum. From his spot on his knees, Xavier stared up at Dean as he swallowed every drop. Dean couldn't look away. "You're so amazing." Even Dean heard the catch in his voice as he whispered the words.

Xavier came to his feet and claimed Dean's mouth. The taste of his own cum coated Dean's tongue. He savored every lick and caress. They were such a beautiful love that Dean wanted to cry and cheer. Xavier made him want to climb a mountain and shout from the highest point. He was the luckiest bastard in the world.

"Marry me. I want to have your babies."

"Shut up," Dean said with a laugh, pushing Xavier away. "You're so ridiculous. How did you get me to fall in love with you?"

Xavier shrugged. "I'm lucky like that. Now get dressed. I want coffee."

Blowing out a sigh, Dean grabbed his bag and dug out his clothes. He dressed quickly before Xavier could attack him again. In truth, Dean wanted to make Xavier fly too, but he knew Xavier was someone not to be fucked with once he started saying he wanted coffee. That meant he had wanted coffee two hours ago and now they were in the danger zone. His baby would always get what he wanted as long as Dean was around. Dean wanted to be with him forever, but he imagined that discussion would have to wait for another day.

XAVIER DIDN'T CARE HE WAS BEING OVER THE TOP and ridiculous today. He was happy. Fuck. He felt free. Xavier hadn't breathed this clearly in ages. But he had to admit, Dean telling him to shut up and pushing him away at his marriage proposal stung a bit. Nonetheless, he let it go. Xavier could admit to himself that he hadn't sounded serious. It was the happiness thing. That had every word he spoke sounding as lighthearted as he felt. He would just have to keep dropping hints as often as possible, so Dean wasn't too shocked when he found himself beneath Xavier's roof. No matter what it took, they would not be sleeping apart again.

They left Dean's surprisingly normal teenage bedroom behind, walking hand in hand through the house. Xavier fought the urge to skip like a little kid.

"Let's take one of Brett's cars. He won't care and I don't have a second helmet with me."

Roman's mom, Peggy, appeared in their path from one of the rooms. "Ooh, where are you boys headed?"

Xavier immediately linked arms with her and dragged her along. He loved Peggy. She was a nut. "We're headed out to get coffee at the gayest coffee shop in town. So I know you're in."

"Damn straight." Peggy was a gay rights activist in her hometown in Colorado. She adopted every gay man she met, and she was exactly the type person Dean needed in his life. Despite her enthusiasm, she didn't look entirely thrilled with Xavier. "Where were you last night, mister? I'm not overjoyed with the fact that you missed my son's wedding."

Xavier drew back, trying to look as offended as possible. "I would never. I was here." He dropped the act. "As to the reception, I totally missed that. I can only tolerate so much of a crowd. Where's your husband this morning and how do I keep missing him?"

Peggy gave a dismissive wave. "He's out playing golf. Brett and Roman went to that sex club they don't think I know about, so I'm all alone."

Dean made a choking sound.

Peggy reached past Xavier and slapped Dean's arm. "Hey there, kiddo. Don't tell me you didn't know your brother is a freak. I've known all about my son for a while. If I can survive that, you can deal." She motioned between them. "I see you two are finally sleeping together. It's about time. I thought the fireworks might take out an eye before you two got it together."

Xavier flashed her a bright smile as he opened the door leading to the garage for everyone. "Oh, sweetie. You're so far behind on the tea. We've been sleeping together for months. The new battle is me trying to get him to marry me or at least move in, but he keeps treating my proposals like a joke."

Dean snorted and shook his head. "Stop."

Xavier motioned Dean's way while keeping up the banter with Peggy. "See? He doesn't take a word I say seriously."

"It's your tone, baby doll. You're all happy and shit. Until you sound serious, he won't know you mean it."

Xavier nodded and helped her into the passenger seat of the Range Rover Dean chose. After closing her door, Xavier circled the car and kissed Dean before climbing into the backseat. Since Dean kept smiling and shaking his head, Xavier couldn't stop doing everything possible to make him smile. While Dean drove them to The Back Porch, Xavier stared at Dean's profile. Peggy chattered happily and Dean kept up his end. Xavier couldn't focus on anything but Dean. He knew Peggy was right. It was his tone. There was still a huge part of Xavier that shied away from getting hurt. That part still remembered what it felt like to be without Dean. He wasn't sure he could take the rejection right now. Even though they were amazing, Xavier knew Dean also walked on eggshells a bit. Xavier recognized Dean also played off Xavier's words as a joke for that reason. He would have to find his moment to be real.

The Back Porch wasn't anywhere near as busy

as usual. Xavier wondered if everyone had stayed so late at the reception getting plastered that no one was up yet for the day. Wrecker motioned for them to sit anywhere while he took someone's order.

"Oh my. Is that who I think it is? Didn't I see him at the wedding too? What is he doing waiting tables?"

Dean explained as they sat. "Wrecker owns the place."

"Ah," Peggy said, sounding relieved. "Don't get me wrong, I don't think there's anything wrong with waiting tables. I've done it. I was just wondering if I needed to start a letter-writing campaign. Being gay shouldn't be a reason for excluding people from playing professional sports."

Dean filled the seat next to Xavier, making Xavier's heart sing. He needed to drape his arm across the back of Dean's chair and stake his claim. His heart demanded it. Xavier leaned over and kissed the tip of Dean's nose. He couldn't help himself.

"You two are so cute. I could just die," Peggy said, looking ready to start clapping like a little kid.

A shadow fell over the table. All eyes turned that way. Milo stood close to Dean, eyeing him intently.

While holding Dean's stare, he nodded Xavier's way. "I'm glad to see you're back where you belong."

Everyone at the table leaned closer. Milo had such a soulful and soft voice; he drew people in when he spoke.

"Thank you." There was no missing the confusion in Dean's tone. It couldn't have been more obvious he didn't understand why Milo spoke to him.

A small smile touched Milo's lips. His silver eyes flashed dangerously. "I was getting worried I would have to kill you. This is better." He walked away as if he hadn't threatened Dean with physical harm.

Dean looked Xavier's way. They smiled. "The foster brother," they said in unison before laughing.

Peggy shook her head while eyeing the room. "It's always the quiet ones. They'll slash your tires every time. Excuse me, boys. I see someone I met last night. I want to say hi." Peggy left them behind.

Xavier saw his chance. He didn't know why it felt like the right time, but it did. Xavier drew Dean closer. Dean's smile hadn't lost an ounce of happiness all morning. Xavier couldn't look away. "I was serious earlier. If you're not ready to get married yet, I understand, but I want you to move in with me. I don't want to sleep another night without you."

Dean blinked. "Oh. Wow. You are serious."

Xavier nodded. Nervousness set in. He genuinely didn't want to be without Dean ever again. Still, he didn't want to scare him away. "I understand if you don't feel like you can trust me yet." Xavier stopped short of swiping his sweaty palms on his jeans, but just barely.

Dean's expression softened. He rubbed Xavier's leg beneath the table. "There's no one I trust more, and I believe in us. We already lost each other once. No way will we let that happen again, but if you need me under your roof full time to prove it, then of course that's what we'll do."

Before Xavier could decide if he should push again on the marriage proposal or hop to his feet and shout his joy, Wrecker appeared. "What can I get started for you two?"

"Oh, we have a third."

At Dean's reluctance, Wrecker motioned behind them. "Your mom ordered over there."

Dean didn't correct Wrecker. Instead, like Xavier, he turned to see where Peggy had gone. She sat with Roscoe and Remington. The pair sat cuddled side by the side. The same as Xavier and Dean. For the first time in Xavier's memory, they wore genuine smiles while Peggy spoke with her hands flying in every direction.

As they turned back to focus on Wrecker, Dean leaned harder into Xavier's side. Xavier gratefully tucked him closer. Dean shook his head. "That's too bad. I hoped she would celebrate with us. We'll both take a black coffee."

With a nod, Wrecker walked away and left them alone. Xavier stared hard at Dean's profile, willing him to look his way and explain himself. Dean kept his gaze stubbornly straight ahead. Xavier couldn't take it. He lightly pinched Dean's side. "Don't ignore me."

A bright smile lit Dean's face as he snorted. "As if anyone could."

"What are we celebrating?"

Dean made a dismissive motion, as if nothing of importance was discussed. "You know, that thing we just talked about."

Xavier swallowed another growl. Two could play this game. "I hope you're not this flippant while we're picking out a honeymoon destination. Traveling as a celebrity is tricky business." Xavier held his breath, expecting Dean to laugh off the idea.

He felt more than saw Dean shrug. "What's halfway between here and Sweden? I failed geography, but I have a mother-in-law to meet."

An immediate lump in Xavier's throat had him

pressing his lips to Dean's cheek. He lingered there. While he imagined they would have a long engagement, since Dean wouldn't likely marry him right away. Dean had still made him happier than he could vocalize. They needed this security probably more than any couple out there. They were too used to being alone. Xavier silently vowed he would never let Dean down.

Xavier finally managed to pull away. "Probably someplace in northeast Canada. If you want to stay in the US, then likely Maine. Otherwise, there's not much of a halfway point but a bunch of water."

Dean nodded. "You know, as a kid, we moved around a lot, living just about everywhere. I've never been to Maine, though. I hear it's nice."

Xavier leaned his elbow on the table and propped his cheek on his fist as he stayed focused on Dean. "That's where I'll take you, then. Tell me everywhere you've lived."

A bright smile lit Dean's face. "Wow. That's a list. Let's see..."

Xavier settled in to listen. He loved the sound of Dean's voice. Xavier doubted he would ever get enough. He couldn't wait to try. They were the happiness he had been searching for at least for the past decade. Xavier wanted to soak all of it in. He wanted to get started on their future. Xavier would give Dean all the happiness. It was fate.

DAWSON SAT IN HIS CAR AND WAITED. HE HAD just pulled into the parking lot at The Back Porch when he saw Dean heading inside with Xavier. It wasn't that he was avoiding Dean. He just didn't want to be in the way. Dawson was always in the way. He had left the wedding early last night, halfway through Xavier and Dean's fight. If Dawson had one talent, it was ducking out when things got heated. The thing was, he liked Dean. It had been a long time since he had a friend. Mostly, that was due to fear of people judging him harshly. Dean hadn't done that.

The night they had camped out on the beach, they had stayed up the entire night talking. Dean had been extremely open about falling in love with someone out of his reach and the insecurities that came with that. Not to mention, his parents had abandoned him, so he always expected everyone would. Dean's honesty had Dawson telling a story he never did. He had told Dean about Milo. About the longing, the love, and the deep shame. There hadn't been any judgment. In fact, Dean had disagreed by pointing out he wasn't truly related to Milo in any way. That didn't matter, though. There was a lot no one understood but him, because no one else could see inside his mind. They didn't know the dark and twisted obsession that lived in his head. No one knew but Milo.

After seeing Dean going inside the coffeehouse, Dawson decided he would wait. Dean wasn't the type to linger all day, drinking coffee. Dawson could hang out in the parking lot until Dean left. Dean deserved to find a happy life with Xavier. He never would if Dawson kept turning up. Plus, it wasn't like Dawson had anything better to do. He pretty much lived at The Back Porch while just trying to make enough money to survive. Today would be no different from any other day.

The driver's side door flew open, startling Dawson. Milo leaned inside and wrapped his arms around Dawson, hugging him against his chest. For a moment, Dawson sat frozen in shock. Then his face turned. His nose automatically sought the crook of Milo's neck, inhaling his light and sweet cologne. Dawson's arms lifted of their own volition and held Milo every bit as tightly. His heartbeat pounded inside his ears. Dawson's chest ached and his eyes stung, because he knew it was only a stolen moment that would haunt him, costing him more than he gained.

Milo's lips lightly brushed the shell of Dawson's ear. A ragged-sounding breath caressed Dawson's skin, making chill bumps skirt down his spine. "I sold another painting of you." He shoved something into Dawson's hand and pulled away. The door closed and it was like Milo had never been there, except for the crippling pain that made it impossible for Dawson to move. He glanced down and uncurled his fingers. It was a sizable chunk of cash. There was a tiny sliver of paper in the middle. Dawson unfolded the bills and the note.

I love you. Pay your rent. Unless you're finally ready to admit you're mine. If so, you know what to do with the money.

Dawson leaned his head back and stared at the ceiling of his car. Even though he hurt so much, he felt like he had the flu, Dawson still smiled. Sometimes, he let himself dream. Maybe today would be the day he would pack up his car and run away with Milo. No one had to know about them. No one at all.

. . .

Keep an eye out for the next Candied Crush, *Beautifully Painted*.

Please consider leaving a review at the retailer where you purchased this book. Reviews really help with a book's visibility, which allows me to continue writing more stories. Thank you, Charity.

ABOUT THE AUTHOR

Charity Parkerson is an award winning and multi-published author with several companies. Born with no filter from her brain to her mouth, she decided to take this odd quirk and insert it in her characters.

*Eight-time Readers' Favorite Award Winner
    *2015 Passionate Plume Award Finalist
    *2013 Reviewers' Choice Award Winner
    *2012 ARRA Finalist for Favorite Paranormal Romance
    *Five-time winner of The Mistress of the Darkpath

Connect with her online:

—Sign up for my newsletter: http://bit.ly/CharityNews
    —Join my readers' group on Facebook: http://bit.ly/CharitysTribe
    —Website: charityparkerson.com

—Facebook:
facebook.com/authorCharityParkerson
facebook.com/TheMenofSin
—Twitter: twitter.com/CharityParkerso
—Instagram: Instagram.com/sinnerauthor